MICHAEL NORTHROP

ROT

TEN

SCHOLASTIC PRESS | NEW YORK

Library of Congress Cataloging-in-Publication Data

Northrop, Michael.
Rotten / Michael Northrop. – 1st ed.
    p. cm.
Summary: When troubled sixteen-year-old Jimmer "JD" Dobbs returns from a mysterious summer "upstate" he finds that his mother has adopted an abused Rottweiler that JD names Johnny Rotten – but soon his tenuous relationship with the dog is threatened.
1. Rottweiler dog – Juvenile fiction. 2. Dogs – Behavior – Juvenile fiction. 3. Juvenile delinquents – Juvenile fiction. 4. Friendship – Juvenile fiction. [1. Rottweiler dog – Fiction. 2. Dogs – Fiction. 3. Juvenile delinquents – Fiction. 4. Friendship – Fiction.]
I. Title.
PZ7.N8185Rot 2013
813.6 – dc23
2012035038

ISBN 978-0-545-49587-5

10 9 8 7 6 5 4 3 2 1   13 14 15 16 17

First edition, April 2013
Printed in the U.S.A.   23

The text type was set in Garamond.
The display type was set in Penumbra.
Book design by Phil Falco

FOR LITTLE BIT AND MAX,
TWO GREAT DOGS, TWO
GOOD BOYS

PART · I

FROM BARK TO BITE

1

The bus heading down from upstate says PETER PAN on the side. It might as well say LOSERS. Everyone on here is some combination of bad adjectives: poor, old, sick, bloated, and worse. I've pegged one as homicidal and another as suicidal. Luckily, they're not sitting next to each other. No one on here is getting the better of things. No one owns a car or can afford a train ticket. I fit right in, a sixteen-year-old being shipped across the state in the middle of the night with absolutely no say in the matter.

I'm staring out the window at headlights, taillights, and streetlights, and I've got double stop signs up. My earbuds are in and the old-school punk music is at maximum volume, and I've got a book on my lap so I can pretend to read, if necessary. It's not. The old guy next to me hasn't said a word, and I think he might have wet himself.

We finally pull into the station in Brantley. This is the last stop for me. I slide by the old dude, maintaining as much airspace as possible. The first word I say to him is "Sorry." Then I stand in the aisle and wait as the line shuffles slowly toward the door. Most of these people are continuing on to an actual city. They just want to buy snacks, smoke, use a real bathroom, or get some air. I don't mind the wait. I'm almost home. I've been counting the days for months, but now I feel more nervous than anything.

The air is warmer out in the parking lot, and I start to come around a little. The compartment doors are open along the side of the bus, and I paw through the luggage until I find my bag. Just to be sure, I give it a quarter turn so I can see the JD in marker on the front. My name is Jimmer Dobbs, but I go by JD if I can help it.

The bag is pretty heavy, but I lift it clear without too much trouble. I take a look around the parking lot, scanning for my mom's Honda, but I don't see it. I pull out my phone and check for a text or a call. There's nothing, so I head inside the station.

I claim one of the orange plastic bucket seats in the waiting area. I check my phone and look around. The station is too big for this dried-up town now. Most of the people here are either from the bus I came in on or they work here.

I'm kind of hungry, but there's a line at the vending machines. The people are looking over their shoulders, afraid the bus is going to leave them here. I check my phone again and wait. It's not like I expected a parade or a party, but I thought my mom would at least be here. I called her once I saw the first exit sign to let her know. The trip in from Stanton is like twenty minutes.

The people get their Snickers or Twix or barbecue potato chips and get back on the bus, and the bus does its part and leaves. Maybe I'll call her again, just to check in. I want to go to the vending machines, but I'm not sure about leaving my bag here and it feels lame to take it with me.

I take it anyway. I'm stranded in a bus station. Lameness is unavoidable, and if I didn't want this stuff, I wouldn't have carted it to the edge of the state and back. I hook the strap over my shoulder and start walking toward the machines. I hear one of the doors *shoosh* open when I'm halfway across the floor. I look over and it's my mom. I change direction and head toward her.

"Hey, baby bird," she says. Mom calls me that sometimes. I wish she wouldn't.

"Hi, Mom," I say, smiling for the first time in recent memory.

We rarely hug, which guarantees that this one will be awkward, and it is.

"Welcome back," she says.

"Whoop-de-doo," I say, spinning my finger in a little circle around the dingy bus station.

We're mostly quiet on the drive home. I've been away all summer, and even though she visited a few times, there's almost too much to catch up on. I don't think either of us really knows where to start.

"There's a surprise for you at home," she says at one point.

She doesn't say why she was late getting to the station, and I don't ask, but this is better: a surprise. I think maybe it's a cake or something. I'm kind of hungry because I never made it to the vending machines. Pretty soon, we pass the sign that says WELCOME TO STANTON! It's only that one line, because there's nothing impressive to add.

Everything after that is the same as when I left: the pizza place, little bridge, so-called downtown, and town green, then the little dip in the road and our boxy white house coming up on the left.

We pull into the driveway, and I brace myself for the pothole at just the right moment. Some things you don't forget. The car comes to a stop and Mom turns it off and drops the keys in her purse. The engine keeps ticking afterward. That's new. I see Mom listening to it, already calculating how much it will end up costing us.

I bang through the side door with my bag, make the right, and head into the front room to drop my stuff. I know the room well, so I don't bother to switch on the light. Sure enough, I slam my shin into something and go down in a heap.

I realize midfall that it must be the coffee table. I realize postfall that Mom must have moved it while I was away. I grab my shin and swear, but my voice is drowned out by the noise suddenly filling the room. It makes even less sense than the table being out of place. I still can't see anything, so for a second I think maybe I'm imagining it or it's coming from the TV. But the TV is off and the sound keeps coming: It's a dog, barking its head off, barking at me. It makes no sense: We don't have a dog. We never have.

I look around the dark room, trying to figure out where it is. It sounds close, and I don't want to get leg humped or mauled or rabies. I reach up and sort of cover my face, so that I'm looking out through my spread fingers. Just as my eyes are beginning to adjust to the dark, the light flips on and I see my mom standing at the edge of the room.

"Don't worry," she says. "He's new."

It takes me a moment to realize she's talking to the dog.

2

I wake up early, like I've had to do all summer, and like I'll have to do when school starts up a week from tomorrow. I turn over on my side and kick my leg out from under the sheet. There's a nice breeze coming in through the window screen, and I start to drift back to sleep. But just as I'm going under, I hear something.

It's a quick beat of footsteps coming up the stairs. At first, I think it must be Mom, but then I hear the dog's nails on the wood. I turn over and face the door. I can hear the clicks getting closer as he heads down the little hallway.

My door is open a crack and I watch the narrow gap as the sound gets closer and stops. The door isn't open wide enough for the dog to get in, but from what I saw last night, it would be no problem for him to push it open. He's built like a cement truck.

After a few seconds, his nose appears in the gap. He pushes it in as far as he can without touching either the door or the frame. He sniffs twice and then pulls his nose back out of sight. More quiet.

Man, I think, that dog definitely got the wrong impression. Normally, this room would be rank enough to repel anything with a functioning sense of smell, but this morning it's all fresh air and clean laundry.

I expect to hear his feet – or paws, I guess – padding back down the hallway, but there's no sound at all. I'm starting to wonder if I dreamed the whole thing, and then: *Bam!* He jams his whole head through the door. It swings open at least a foot, giving him enough space to turn and look at me.

Holy crap.

His head is like a black-and-brown cinder block. The top is all black, except for two little brown dots, one over each eye. They sort of make it look like he's thinking bad thoughts. The muzzle is all brown, except for a black stripe on top, which leads down to his black nose and black mouth. His jaws look insanely powerful, like Mom had adopted an alligator.

I remind myself of how skittish he was last night, how he went and hid behind Mom. He'd been all big talk in the dark: *Bark! Bark! Bark!* But as soon as the lights came on, he ran out into the hall like a two-year-old, looking back at me from behind her legs, with his head held low. He was literally all bark and no bite.

So I'm telling myself what my mom told me: that he's just a dog, a rescue dog that's still afraid of people. But looking at his face now, I can't tell what he's thinking. We're just looking at each other. I watch the skin bunch up and shift around his eyes as he watches me – even his face has muscles.

He swipes a thick pink tongue across the side of his upper jaw. It lifts the gummy black skin around his mouth, and for a split second, I see the flash of one extra-long white tooth. I guess that's what they call a canine tooth. He pulls his head back out of the room and disappears. A moment later, I hear him heading down the hallway. He pauses at the landing, then avalanches down the stairs.

I let out a long, slow breath. That was weird — and that was a big frickin' tooth! There's no way I'm getting back to sleep now. I throw the sheet off and get up. I open the top drawer of my dresser and look at row after row of clean socks and underwear. It looks like a picture in a catalog — and not a catalog I'd shop from.

I pick out my outfit and get dressed. My jeans feel tight, like they always do after they've been washed. My black T-shirt feels so crisp, I wonder if it's been replaced with a new one. It's a clean start for my clothes — and maybe for that dog — but that's about it. Today is the day I return to my regularly scheduled life, already in progress, not going so great.

3

Sometimes I get my breakfast and take it to the front room, but it feels like I should eat it here with Mom this morning. It's been a long time since we've done anything like that. I'm pretty sure she's thinking the same thing, because she's cooking, which she doesn't usually do in the morning. Or maybe not cooking, exactly. She's making toast. She is toasting, but that's also rare.

She watches the toast pop up and then plucks it out without waiting, making a funny hot-hot-hot expression. She brings my toast over on a little plate and it's exactly how I like it: white bread, medium dark, with plenty of butter. As she puts two more pieces in the ancient toaster, I get up to get my cereal.

I wonder if it's going to be the same box from before I left, but it's a new one. I pull hard on the plastic bag inside, and it bursts open, spilling cereal all over the counter. Meanwhile, my toast is getting cold and hers isn't done yet. The timing feels off. We're both trying too hard.

Finally, we're both sitting down at the small kitchen table with our breakfast in front of us. She has her coffee and I have my Coke and it seems like someone should say something.

"So," I start.

"Bon appétit!" she says, making fun of her grand, toasted gesture.

"It's good," I say, but my timing is off again, and I say it before taking a bite of the toast instead of after.

We don't say anything for a while after that. I wonder if she can hear me chewing my cereal or if that's only loud inside my head.

"I got you new cereal," she says.

"I saw that," I say. "I don't think that stuff goes bad, like, ever."

And that was the wrong thing to say again because it's like I don't appreciate it, and I know that cereal is expensive.

"No sense risking it!" I add.

She looks at me over her coffee mug, and then we both go back to eating. She's just sort of nibbling at her toast, and I notice there's no butter on it. Is she watching her cholesterol or something? Did she have a checkup? Was it bad news? She has some gray hairs now. I can see them in the bright light coming through the window.

I'm trying to think of something to say when I hear that sound again. The dog comes in from the living room, and when he hits the linoleum, he click-clacks for a few steps. I think he must extend his nails for grip sometimes. I guess maybe he's still getting used to the different rooms.

He shoots past my side of the table, giving me a quick look. He doesn't seem scary here, in bright daylight in the kitchen, and he's the opposite of aggressive. If he had a tail instead of a little stump, it would be between his legs. But he straightens up and his head rises back to normal height as he reaches Mom.

She stands up and he follows her over to the window. There's a small glass jar there, and I can see now that it's full of dog biscuits. They're red and green and brown. When I came in, I just thought it was a decoration, but I see that they're shaped like little cartoon bones.

Mom pulls the top off, and the dog does this little hop on his back legs, like he's dancing. His mouth is hanging open, and I can actually see the drool beginning to pool around the edges. Mom pulls out a green biscuit and looks over at me. "Do you want to give it to him?"

I watch a fat drop of slobber drip from his mouth to the floor and say, "Nah, you go ahead."

"Are you sure?" she says.

The dog does another little hop. He's staring up at the biscuit and making this weird noise in the back of his throat, and it's like, Just give him the biscuit already, you know? And she does: She drops it and he jumps up — not a hop this time, a real jump — and snatches it out of the air.

It reminds me of a program called *Air Jaws* that I saw during Shark Week, about those great white sharks that shoot themselves out of the water to get the seals. By the time he lands, he's already chewing. It's pretty much the opposite of Mom's nibbling. A few chomps later, the biscuit is gone and he's mopping the tile with his tongue, retrieving the chunks and crumbs that escaped the initial assault.

"Whoa!" I say.

"Yeah," says Mom. "He never had biscuits before."

It takes me a moment to process that last part and then it's kind of a punch in the heart. I mean, that's pretty sucky if you're a dog.

And if he never got biscuits, he probably never got petted or anything like that. But just as I'm thinking that, he gives me another sideways, head-low look, like: Screw you. It's like he knows I'm feeling sorry for him and won't have any of it.

He looks back up at my mom to see if maybe there's another biscuit in his future, but she's already put the top back on the jar, so he just trots back out of the room. His footsteps disappear once he hits the rug, but a few seconds after that, I hear something fall over on the other side of the room.

Mom sits down again, but now at least we have something new to talk about.

"So what's his name, again?" I say. "Jaws?"

"No," she says, laughing. "He just has a sweet tooth — like you!"

I look down at my cereal. The Crunch Berries have turned the milk an unmanly shade of pinkish purple. Can't argue with that.

"His name is Jon-Jon," she adds, remembering the question.

"What?" I say. "Like the piper's son?"

"I think that's Tom Tom," she says. She may be right about that.

"He doesn't look like a Jon-Jon to me."

"Well, I suppose we could call him something else," she says. "I don't think he would miss that old name much." The name or the memories, she means.

"Whatever," I say. "Your dog now."

"I kind of thought he'd be both of ours," she says. "His last owner kept him chained to a tree outside. I don't think he'd mind joint custody in a nice warm house."

I look at her. "Really?" I say. I'm talking half about the tree thing and half about the joint custody, but I can already tell she's serious about both. I've never had part ownership of a dog before. I brought home a frog once when I was really little, but I didn't know how to take care of it and it didn't last three days. "What kind of dog is it anyway? Is he?"

"He's a Rottweiler," she says.

I'm done with my cereal and drinking the multicolored milk. "What is that," I say, lowering my bowl, "German for weird-ass-looking dog?"

"He's not weird," she says, acting offended. "He's handsome!"

"Jon-Jon the Rottweiler," I say, and just like that, it comes to me. I put down my empty bowl. "Johnny Rotten," I say.

Johnny Rotten was the lead singer of the Sex Pistols. They were the first big punk band and pretty much the reason some people still stick safety pins in their noses, ears, or general facial regions. That's when you know you're a good band, when you can get people to do stuff like that. I just listen to the music and wear black boots sometimes. Anyway, it's an awesome name, and I'm kind of proud of myself for thinking of it. Mom's not convinced.

"Oh, I don't know," says Mom. "It sounds so mean."

"Exactly," I say. "Have you seen that thing's teeth?"

She makes a sour expression. "And he wasn't a very good singer, you know? Not really."

I don't like it when Mom talks music with me. It's annoying. And anyway, I think the Sex Pistols are really good: "I am an Antichrist / I am an anarchist!" It's like those are practically the same word, but they mean completely different things. I like that kind of stuff. All the tests say I'm more "verbal."

"Well, that's perfect, then," I say. "Because I don't think this dog can sing, either."

Mom tries to keep the frown on her face, but the corners of her mouth tip up and she smiles.

The good mood lasts until I get up and head toward the door.

4

"Going to see Rudy," I say. My voice is like I'm apologizing.

"Mm-hmm," says Mom, not really looking at me.

It feels like there should be something more, but there's not. Mom may not want me to hang out with my friends, to go back to all of that, but what's the alternative, locking myself in the basement? I push through the front door and let the warm, bright air smack me in the face. Halfway across the front lawn, I pull out my phone and reread Rudy's last text. He's downtown already, probably out behind the CVS. I type with one hand: **On my way \m/**

I have to walk. One of the great indignities of being away all summer is that my learner's permit hasn't had a chance to emerge from its cocoon as a license. I'm in the bike lane, and a green minivan blows by me, doing about sixty and kicking up a plume of dust and dirt. A little chunk of something, a pebble maybe, whizzes past my head. I hear another car coming and take a few steps up onto the Franciscos' lawn until it passes.

The CVS is the center of things downtown, the only recognizable brand we've got now that the Subway closed. I stop and look around once I reach it. I'm half looking for Rudy and half checking to see if there's anything new in town. The verdict: Rudy's not there, and there's never anything new around here.

This town excels at the old, though. As if to prove the point, Mr. Jesperson bangs through the front door of the CVS with a copy of the *Stanton Standard* under one arm and a CVS bag in one hand. The bag looks ready to burst, and I figure it must contain all the pills he has to take to continue to function at his age.

"Jimmer!" he says, spotting me as we head toward each other on the walkway.

"Hi, Mr. J.," I say. I've always called him that, because when I first met him, I was too young to manage *Jesperson*.

"Where you been?" he says. "Haven't seen you around hardly at all."

I can feel my eyes narrow, and for a second I think maybe he's screwing with me, like he knows exactly where I've been and he's just making me say it. But then I get a grip. Mr. J. isn't giving me a hard time. He hasn't given me trouble even once in his very long life. But he's looking at me, waiting for an answer.

"Aw, you know," I say. "I am a man of mystery."

That's either good enough for him or he realizes that's all he's going to get. He looks down and begins rummaging through the overstuffed bag in his hand. Oh no, I think. Please, for the love of all that is not impossibly lame, no. But, yes, he's searching through his bag for candy. He's going to give me candy, like I'm still five years old and can't say his name. And he's going to do it right here on this walkway in the absolute center of town. I look around to see if anyone is coming, and of course they are. The sidewalks are getting busier. There's a stream of dressed-up families empty-ing out of the church at the end of the block.

It takes him forever. Even when he finds the little plastic bag of candy, he still has to open it. I watch the veins shift and the liver spots stretch as he maneuvers the bag and pinches its top. People are passing us on either side, nodding at Jesperson, who they all know and trust. I'm sure they wonder why he's wasting his time on me.

"That's OK," I say. "Really."

"No, no," he says. "You always loved these things."

They're butterscotch hard candies. They're one of those old people's candies, like gumdrops, but it's true, I loved them — when I was five.

"Can I . . ." I start, but it doesn't seem like I should say "help," for some reason. "Do you want me to . . ."

Finally, the bag pops open — and he gives me one piece! All that, and I get one piece. I mean, I don't like them as much as I used to, but all that for one butterscotch?

"Thanks," I say, more for the effort than the candy. His face is red from wrestling with the bag, and I imagine him sitting alone later, dentures out and slowly chain-sucking the rest of the but-terscotches to death.

Normally I'd walk through the CVS now. That's where I was headed, but I feel like I've interacted with the general population enough at this point, so I turn and walk around the side of the building. Sure enough, there's Rudy Binsen, my best friend since forever. He's wearing a T-shirt that says HANG OUT WITH YOUR WANG OUT and sitting on the old, beat-up bench, on the side farthest from the garbage can.

"What're you eating?" he says when he sees me.

"Butterscotch," I say.

So that's it, the first words we've said to each other all summer. I sit down on the bench, not too close to him but not too far away either, because there are four or five bees buzzing around the top of the garbage can on this side.

"Geez, man," says Rudy. "It's been forever."

"Seriously," I say. I look over at him. "Nice shirt. Solid advice." Shirts like that are kind of his thing, but I haven't seen this one before.

"Wearing my Sunday best," he says. "So how was 'upstate'?"

He actually makes the air quotes with his fingers. I ignore them.

"OK," I say. "Boring."

"Yeah, right. Because you were 'at your aunt's house' or whatever?"

He doesn't make the air quotes this time, but I can hear them.

"Yeah," I say, trying to sound casual.

"Dude, that's ridiculous. They don't 'send you to the country' when you already live in the middle of nowhere."

I look up at the sky. It took, what, thirty seconds for us to get into this again? "Yeah," I say, "but this was, like, the turbosticks: no Internet — my aunt doesn't even have a cell phone."

"Yeah, more like everyone up there is *in* a cell," he says, then laughs at his own joke.

"Mom thought it would be good for me," I say. "Get me away from all the bad influences around here."

He makes a fake wounded expression, like I've hurt his feelings.

"You seen Janie?" he asks after a while.

Perfect, I think, the only topic more uncomfortable than the last one.

"Nah," I say. I want to stop there, but I can't help myself. "Is she, you know? Is there someone . . ."

"You mean someone else?" he says.

"Dude, man, I don't even know," I say. "I don't know if 'someone else' really enters into it at this point. I just mean, is she, like, seeing anyone?"

Rudy looks over at me for a second. I know him, so I know that he's thinking about making a joke, maybe something about "entering into it." But he thinks better of it, because he knows me, too. "I don't think so," he says, shrugging. "And I haven't seen anything online."

"Yeah, OK," I say. I'm sort of wondering if that means he was checking out her profile, but I guess he might mean in his news feed. We all have "mutual friends," even if we don't necessarily like them. "I just thought you might've heard something."

"Nope," says Rudy. "You should just call her or something."

Which is obviously true, but I haven't yet. The last time we talked, it didn't go so well. Which is like driving a car into a train and calling it a wrong turn. "Yeah," I say. "Hey, speaking of all that" – I wave my hand around to show that I'm talking about more than one person now – "I haven't updated my status or anything. So don't tell anyone I'm back yet, OK? I need to get my bearings or whatever."

"Well, that's too bad," says Rudy. "Because it's too late."

"Who'd you tell?" I say.

"Mars," he says, holding up his phone. "Right before you got here."

"Yeah, Mars." That's Dominic DiMartino. "So Aaron will know, too."

"Yeah, probably. What's the big deal? Those guys are cool. You know, usually."

"Yeah, yeah, course," I say.

"I've been hanging with them a lot," he says. "Not like you've been around."

"Yeah, yeah, I know. It's cool."

"Well, I don't know why you're being a freak, but I think we're supposed to head over to Brantley tomorrow. You in?"

"Not sure I can handle the excitement," I say.

"Seriously, man . . ."

"Yeah . . . Course . . . What time?"

"Don't know . . . I'll text you."

"Cool, cool," I say.

We just talk for a while after that, and he catches me up on some of the nothing that happened around here. We roam around downtown a little, because there's only a little of it to roam around. Then I tell him I have to go.

"Sure, man," he says.

"It's good to see you, man."

"Yeah, you, too."

And it is good to see him. It's good to talk to him, and I sort of feel like he let me off the hook easy and we're pretty much back to normal. So that's all good, but I feel uneasy and on edge as I head back home. Brantley tomorrow, with all of them . . . It's like I haven't been gone at all.

I guess that's the problem.

5

I walk home the back way, along the bike path through the woods. It's quieter, and you don't feel like as much of a second-class citizen as you do walking along the side of the road. About halfway, there's a tree that sort of leans out into the path. It's bent like an elbow, and when I was a little kid, I had to jump to touch the part where it bends. Today, I just reach my hand out and slap it as I pass. It's a tradition.

Walking that way, I come home by the backyard. Even before I get there, I can see that the fence has been patched up. You can still see the old holes through the new wire, and I wonder why Mom had it done. Then I notice that the grass is a lot longer than usual, and I suddenly realize what it's hiding. Mom must let the dog do his business out here.

The grass is like eight or ten inches high in the center and slopes down to a few bare patches near the posts. The fence is barely waist high, and normally I'd hop it and go in the back door. But I just walk by. The grass has been mined, and the corners have been dug up and pissed to death.

I walk around and go in the front door. I'm a little distracted, thinking about a few things that Rudy said and about that trip to

Brantley tomorrow, but I sort of snap back to reality as I turn the door handle. I remember the big, barking commotion last night. I push the door open anyway because, you know, I live here. There are two quick barks, but that's it. As soon as he sees who it is, he turns and starts slinking back out of the kitchen. Just to test something, I say: "What up, dog?"

As I suspected, it just makes him slink faster. Once he's gone, I realize I forgot to tell Rudy about this dog. I'm not sure why. Nervous, I guess. It's not like I had any other news to share — and he'd at least appreciate the name. He was a big fan of my last pet, that dead frog, Mr. Hops, croaked on a Thursday. RIP, little fella: Rot in Place.

As I'm heading toward the front room, I can hear Mom coming down the stairs. Maybe she was just up there getting the laundry, I tell myself, but it's also possible she was going through my stuff. She makes it up to me later by bringing in pizza rolls while I'm camped out on the couch, watching preseason football.

"What is it, a holiday?" I say, sitting up to take the plate.

She bats me on the head. "Careful," she says. "They're hot."

"OK," I say, moving my head from side to side to point out that she's in between me and the TV. It's Texans versus Rams, so I don't have a rooting interest, but it's a pretty good game, and the front room is sort of my territory. At least that's the way I see it. She's still standing there. For a second, I think: Uh-oh, she found something in my stuff. But then I remember there wasn't anything in my stuff. Finally, I figure it out.

"Thanks, Mom," I say.

"You're welcome, baby bird," she says, and turns and walks away.

If anyone else called me that, I would literally, physically kill them. With a dull spoon. As it is, I reach for a pizza roll.

"Hot!" she says as she exits the room, her back still to me.

I have no idea how she does that, but I drop it back on the plate. It didn't feel too hot, but it's the insides that'll get you with those things, so I watch the game for a while. A few minutes later, I grab a pizza roll and pop it in my mouth. It's just the right temperature: warm but not blistering. When I look back up, I see the dog looking at me.

Once again, it's just his head. He's in the hall, kind of poking his face into the room. I feel like telling him to man up — or dog up, maybe — but he's built more solidly than half the guys the Rams are currently trotting out on defense, so I guess I should be careful what I wish for. As it turns out, he's not looking at me after all.

I follow his eyes and he's staring at the plate. The way he hopped around for those biscuits this morning, I should've known. "You're a real chowhound, huh?" I say. This time, he doesn't slink away. He turns his head a little, sort of dipping his left ear toward the floor, and looks at me. The little brown dot above each eye makes him look like he's thinking about something much more profound than processed, microwaved food.

"You want a pizza roll?" I ask. "Are you even allowed?"

He doesn't answer, but he tips his head back the other way — right ear toward the floor — when I say "pizza roll," so I think he was at least able to identify the noun. I heard somewhere that chocolate is bad for dogs, but I'm not sure about the rest of the vast kingdom of junk food.

He takes two small steps forward. Now his shoulders are in the room. I raise my hand and he takes a step back, but he stops once he sees that I'm just reaching for the plate. I hear something happen on the TV – a Texan touchdown, probably – but I don't look. I feel like if I look away, he'll vanish.

Instead, I hold up a pizza roll, and he very slowly, very cautiously takes a few more steps forward. He's all the way in the room now, and I'm pretty sure that, food or not, that's as close as he's going to come. I flick my wrist and toss the little tan roll to him. Just like with the biscuit, he rises up on his hind legs and snatches it out of the air. He catches it in the side of his mouth. He's already chewing by the time he lands, but a pizza roll being what it is, a glob of red filling pops out the side and lands on the floor.

He finishes gobbling down the roll and looks down at the filling, ears up, legitimately surprised. I don't think he's ever eaten something with filling before. He must be a quick learner, though, because he dips his head down and licks it up in three quick swipes of his tongue. He raises his head up and looks tremendously pleased with this whole turn of events.

Then he looks at me and starts making that weird noise in the back of his throat. I toss him another one. Once again, he Air Jaws it. This time, no filling escapes, but he still looks around for it when he's done. Maybe he's not as fast a learner as I thought. While he's sniffing the floor, I pop the last one in my mouth.

"You snooze, you lose, boy," I say.

I hold up my hands to show him that they're empty.

"No more," I say. "You cleaned me out."

He looks at my hands, looks at the plate, then turns and walks out of the room. He doesn't even say thank you.

After the game's over, I pick up my phone and go looking for the dog. I find him in the living room. The living room is also the dining room because it's just off the kitchen and the house isn't that big anyway. JR has staked out a spot in the corner. His eyes follow me, but he doesn't move one way or the other. I point my phone at him. "Pizza roll," I say.

He looks up and I snap a picture. I head back to the front room and send the pic and a quick text message to Rudy: **Forgot 2 tell u, got a dog. Name is Johnny Rotten & looks like this.**

I get a text back: **Rawk! \m/**

A few minutes after that, he sends another one: **Must meet dog. Maybe start band?**

I think that's pretty funny. Can you imagine?

No problem, I type. I figure there's already enough going on tomorrow, so I add: **Tuesday?**

Rudy's reply is just **\m/** — the devil horns always mean yes. I didn't mention that the dog is completely neurotic, but I guess he can find that out for himself.

6

It's Monday. In a week, Mondays will suck because of school. Today might suck too, but that will be self-inflicted.

Mom has already left for work by the time I get up. I stumble around the empty kitchen, and I can tell what she had for breakfast by the dishes in the sink. It always sort of reminds me of a zombie movie: the house empty, but with signs that people had been there recently ("This toaster is still warm!"). I sit there eating my cereal and start to wonder where the dog is.

I get up and take the lid off the biscuit jar. Sure enough, as soon as he hears the sound of glass clinking off glass, he appears like a drooling genie. I take out a red biscuit, because that seems like the coolest color. He starts twitching, and his eyes get wide and follow every movement I make. It's like my hand is remote controlling his head.

But he doesn't come any closer. He wants me to throw it to him again. It's like an agreement between us: He'll take food from me as long as I don't get too close. I toss the biscuit high this time. He leans back and gathers his legs directly under himself like a kangaroo, then springs straight up and vacuums the thing out of the sky.

He waits to see if I'll give him another one. I bet Mom gave him one too, so he's already in the bonus round. It's pretty clear that he'd eat these things all day long if he could find enough suckers to feed them to him. I sniff my hand to see if the biscuits really smell that good. They don't, but they don't smell that bad, either. By the time I put the top on the jar and turn back around, he's gone. Still, I finish my cereal thinking that, technically, I didn't have breakfast alone.

There's a note on the counter: *Let JJ out back if he needs to go. Don't give him any more biscuits!* I pull open the junk drawer and push through the tape and batteries and stuff until I find the marker. Then I cross out *JJ* and put *JR*. I'm not sure what to do about the "needs to go" thing, though.

I'm going to be gone all day, which Mom doesn't know and doesn't need to. I'll be home before she is, and that right there is the main reason she has to trust me. She might not want me to hang around with those guys, but she can't lock me in or really keep track of me when I'm out. It's true now and it will be just as true once school starts.

I decide to leave the back door open a little. That way, he can go if he needs to. I guess it's a "security risk," but this is a pretty small town, so that's not much of a problem here. People mostly know their neighbors and keep an eye on things, and if all else fails, a lot of them own guns. We don't have one, but Mom got an NRA sticker from someone and stuck it on our door, right above a sticker for a security system that we also don't really have.

Anyway, add it all up and there aren't a lot of break-ins. The ones that make it into the always-entertaining Police Blotter in the *Standard* are mostly things like someone's ex-boyfriend breaking in "under the influence" to take his bowling ball back. We don't have any bowling balls to steal, and in addition to our fierce array of stickers, we have a shiny new Rottweiler. He's been a total wuss so far, but I figure the barking and the sheer size of his jaws should be enough.

Anyway, I leave the back door most of the way open and the screen door open a crack. JR is curled up in the same place as yesterday, sleeping off all those biscuits. "Just push through if you need to go," I say when I pass him. "*Do not* crap on the floor!"

He lifts his eyes but not his head, and I'm not entirely reassured.

I wait out front for the guys. I figure Aaron will be driving, and I'm right. I figure he'll be a little late, and I'm right about that, too. At not quite a quarter past ten, his big boat of a Chevy Malibu pulls to a stop along the curb. I hop up off the grass and get in the backseat, alongside Rudy.

"Hi, girls," I say, once the car starts rolling.

They each insult me in their own way. Rudy's is the best. For a second, I'm not even sure what a "whoremonger" is, but I think it through and decide it means "pimp." In these circles, that's a compliment.

We have the windows up because the AC is on, but it's barely working, so it's still pretty hot in here. It's the first time all four of us have been together in months, and you can sense the energy instantly: four dudes in a car, late summer. We steer clear of serious topics for the first few miles, but as we're leaving town, Aaron says, "I ran into Janie the other day."

"Oh yeah?" I say, "How, uh, how's she doing?"

The car is silent for a few seconds. It's just the sound of the wheels and the AC as they register the fact that I don't know. I shouldn't have said that.

"Seemed OK," says Aaron, his tone even and unreadable. Aaron Vandever is always in total control.

"More like *who's* she doing!" blurts Mars, like he can't hold it in any longer. For a second, I wonder if he knows something. Then he says, "She was over at my place last night," and I know he doesn't. He doesn't stop, though. "And it was a *long* night!"

"Drop dead, Mars," I say. Sometimes Mars is really funny, but this isn't one of those times.

"Don't worry," he says. "I gave her what she needed." He turns back toward me and we make sort of glancing eye contact. I'm glaring at him, but his eyes are darting all over the place, and I'm not sure the message really gets through. If Mars hasn't been officially diagnosed with ADHD or anything like that yet, I'll do it right now. He's always been a little out of control. He's the opposite of Aaron, and in a weird way, I think that's why they get along so well.

I can see Aaron in the rearview mirror: His eyes are on the road, but he's smiling. He's not going to do anything about this. Mars turns back around and I'm thinking: If he says one more thing about Janie, I'm going to punch him in the back of the head. I think he's about to, but Rudy steps in. "So dick weed here got a dog," he says.

"You got a job?" says Mars. Either he misheard or he's still being a jerk. "That sucks!"

"Hold on, Mars," says Aaron. "I want to hear this."

Mars finally shuts up.

"You got a dog, man?" says Aaron.

"Uh, yeah," I say. "My mom did, but he's, like, half mine."

It's always dicey to mention your mom around these guys, but Aaron lets it slide.

"He?"

"Yeah," I say, "he's a dude. . . . Or at least, he used to be."

We all grimace in fake pain, and Rudy sort of hisses through his teeth, because that's not something you even want to think about.

"What kind of dog?" says Aaron.

"He's a Rottweiler," I say. "He's built like a, I don't know, a battleship or something."

"Is that like a pit bull?" says Mars.

"Bigger," I say. "And blacker."

"Too black, too strong!" blurts Mars, who is neither.

"He dangerous?" Aaron asks.

"Only if you're a biscuit," I say, and everyone laughs. Mars laughs too, and not a fake laugh either. I feel sort of bad that I was about to punch him, but not too bad: I'm sure I'll want to smack him again before the day is over. Anyway, I have one more thing to add. "His name is Johnny Rotten."

"Nice," says Rudy, even though he already knew that.

" 'Cause he's a Rottweiler," says Mars, because everyone's mind works at its own pace.

Finally, Aaron weighs in. "Cool," he says, so that's the official word on that.

Aaron turns the stereo on and up, starting with a good, seri- ously hardcore song, and at the speed he's driving, we cover five miles listening to it. Once it's over, he turns the volume down, and I think: This is it. Here it comes. My nerves spike.

I expect them to grill me about my summer, but they don't. I don't know why. It's not like I have any way to escape. I have my story all set and ready to go, though, and I think they know that. We went through the same thing before I left, and I'm sure Rudy told them I haven't changed my story. They've seen all the same war movies as me, so they know that you don't make a direct assault on a defended position, not if you can help it. That's just basic strategy.

Anyway, apart from a few words here and there, we just drive on as if nothing's different, as if I'd seen them all yesterday instead of months ago. "Think we should crack open the win- dows?" I ask as we hit a wide-open stretch between towns.

"Yeah, might as well," says Aaron, knowing that his AC isn't cutting it.

"Better do it before someone lets one go," says Mars.

"I'm amazed we've made it this far," says Rudy.

The windows slide all the way down, and the summer air comes whipping in. That ends the conversation, at least until Brantley. If we want to say something now, we'll have to yell. I lean back and relax a little. In the seat next to me, I'm pretty sure Rudy lets one rip.

7

We park on a side street near the 7-Eleven and climb out into another hot, hazy day. The air is different in Brantley. I can't say exactly why, but then Mars says, "Smells like butt sweat," and I guess that sums it up pretty well.

We fall into formation, two by two, as usual. Aaron and Mars are in front, and Rudy and I are hanging back a little. Mars starts clowning around and ape-walking. He's actually really good at it. Instead of just bending his knees to get low, he bows his legs way out to the sides like a real ape. Then he leans forward and gets his knuckles nearly down to the ground.

We have this stretch of sidewalk to ourselves, and Mars starts giving it the full "Ooh-ooh-aah-aah" treatment. By the end of the block, Aaron is red faced from laughing, and Rudy and I are smiling and shaking our heads. From back here, I can really see the differences in size between us.

In ape terms, Mars is definitely a chimp: small and always chattering. Aaron is a gorilla: big, solid, and mostly quiet, at least when he's not cracking up at one of Mars's stunts. Rudy and I are orangutans, I guess: too tall for chimps, not broad enough for gorillas, and with stretched-out limbs we're both hoping to grow into someday soon.

We turn the corner on to a busier street. Mars straightens up and our smiles flatten into hard, straight lines. Halfway down the block, we push through the doors of the 7-Eleven. I'm third in, behind Mars and in front of Rudy. The girl behind the counter is watching us file in. The place is pretty empty – midmorning – and we make her nervous. She sees the apes in us, too. I give her a little nod. I mean it like, Don't worry about us, but I guess it could mean anything.

We fill our hands with cheap, sugary junk. Rudy and Aaron get coffees and basically make milk shakes out of them with sugar and half-and-half, and Mars and I get Slurpees, because that's why God put 7-Elevens on this earth. I hang back and pay last. Mars shorts the girl. His stuff comes to $5.17, and he tosses a crumpled five on the counter and is out the door by the time she has it halfway flattened out.

"Hey!" she says, shouting at the closing door and the space where he was. She's missing a tooth, off to the side.

"I got it," I say and throw down a crumpled five of my own.

I'm the last one in the store with her, and she looks at me. She's not much older than I am, but you can see she's been through the wringer. Her hands and eyes move a little too much, with those extra flutters and twitches.

"Geez," she says, flattening out the five. "I need an iron for you guys."

"And seventeen cents," I say.

She smiles with her mouth closed, hiding the missing tooth.

Mine comes to $4.67, and I tell her to keep the change. That's the seventeen cents plus some.

"Wow," she says. "Maybe I'll close up early." But I'm already heading toward the door. I'm not looking to make friends or anything. I just don't want any trouble right now.

I find the guys out front. There's nothing to sit on — no town in its right mind would allow a bench in front of a 7-Eleven — so they're all sitting on a little square of grass alongside the store. I find a spot and get to work fueling up. We sit there, crunching and chewing and slurping. We do it fast because we really are like animals down here, sitting on the ground, eating crap.

I see Rudy fold a giant Slim Jim back on itself, doubling it up and eating it in three or four big bites. Mars has taken the top off his Slurpee and is drinking it that way, cherry-red clown lips forming around his mouth. An old couple walks by, and we watch them the whole time, sort of daring them to look over. They've been alive long enough to know better.

Five minutes later, we're back up and moving. I can feel the sugar in my veins and the sun on my face, and it's the same for the others. Rudy gives us a little bass line as we walk: "Waanta-waantaah-wakka-waaaah!" It's like the soundtrack to the movie of our lives.

We hear the skateboards coming, two blocks away. The sound is unmistakable, and we sort of get ready. I see Rudy make a quick fist and let it go, as a little jolt of adrenaline hits my system. We were in a fight once: four of us, four of them. It was a totally fair fight, until it became clear that it wasn't. Anyway, it started because of a skateboard.

But this time, it's just two little kids. The electric charge fades from the air, and a wave of relief washes over me. The kids see us and slow down. Then the one in front speeds back up and the smaller one follows him. Ten or twelve feet away, the first one executes a halfway decent ollie.

"Yeah!" says Aaron.

"There ya go!" says Rudy.

Everyone who's skated remembers their first ollie, their first board slide and boneless. I give the kid a little whistle and he rolls by smiling, his cheeks turning red as he goes. Then it's the second kid's turn. He's younger, and he tries a board slide on the curb and totally eats it.

"Oh damn!" says Rudy.

It's quiet for a few seconds. We're all waiting to see if the kid's going to get up laughing or crying or at all. I hear the sound of the first kid turning his board around. Finally, the second kid gets up and gives us this incredibly dorky thumbs-up. You can see the pain on his face — he's just barely holding it together — but that thumbs-up is too much and we all bust out laughing. Then he makes a show of walking over to the curb. He leans down and touches some imaginary notch or bump, as if that's why he wound up in the road.

"Keep it up, kid," says Aaron.

"Next time I see you," says Mars, "I want a three-sixty."

We don't really expect the kid to say anything, and we're

already moving again, but here comes this little voice: "Tre or pop shove-it?"

Those are the two main kinds of 360, and it's just so hilarious to hear this kid say that after totally eating it on an easy board slide that we nearly end up on the ground ourselves. We laugh for, like, two blocks, but we pull it together by the time we reach the liquor store.

8

You might think a semiskeezy place like Liquor Mania — right on the main drag and exposed to every set of eyes this town can muster — is not the place for someone looking to avoid unnecessary trouble. Especially if that someone is sixteen. And you'd be right, but I don't even have to go in. All I have to do is wait outside while Aaron goes in and tries his fake ID.

Aaron is seventeen already and looks even older than that. His fake ID is top of the line, too, but you don't want the guy behind the counter to see a bunch of obviously underage dudes waiting outside for their friend. So we make ourselves scarce. There's a bench outside the post office, just down the street. Rudy and I sit on it and plaster these responsible-citizen looks on our faces. The goal is to look friendly and positive without looking deranged or stoned. Rudy's T-shirt features skeletons arranged in all the major sexual positions, so it's a fine line.

Meanwhile, Mars goes into the post office to check out the wanted posters. They have, like, a wall calendar of the FBI's most wanted in there. The post office in Stanton is too small to have one, so Mars likes to check it out when we come here. It's not really a calendar, it's just that it's one page after another, so you have to flip through and look at them one at a time. It lists their names, their crimes, "known aliases," and things like that. It's actually pretty cool.

Anyway, Rudy and I take the opportunity to talk about him. "Man," I say, "I was about to smack him in the head on the ride over."

"Yeah," says Rudy. "Saw that."

"Was he this bad before?" I say.

"Before what?"

"Before, you know, before I went away," I say.

"Yeah, I know," says Rudy. "I was just being a jerk."

"Yeah, should've known."

"How?" says Rudy, setting up one of our standard jokes.

"Your lips were moving."

"Yep," he says. "Anyway, the answer is yes, he's always been like that. You just didn't used to be so defensive."

I nod. It's true.

And then, speak of the devil, Mars comes bounding down the stairs, all full of secondhand criminality. "He out yet?" he asks.

Our eyes have been on the door of the store pretty much the whole time, so we don't have to look over to answer. "Not yet," says Rudy.

"Well, that's a good sign, right?"

"Could be," I say.

"Don't be so negative, man," he says.

"What?" I say. "I wasn't."

A minute later, Aaron pushes his way out the door, empty-handed.

"Dammit," we all say, or words to that effect.

Aaron spots us and walks over. "Guy's a jerk," he says.

For a while, it seems like that's all he's going to say, and it pretty well sums it up. Depending on who you ask, there is either a special place in heaven or a special ring of hell for liquor store workers who do their job honestly. But then he adds, "They've got these sweet two-liter jugs of vodka, dirt cheap."

None of us says anything; we are devastated by our loss. That is the absolute top of the charts for us: cheap, strong, and clear, so you can mix it with anything. Beer is in last place: bulkier, weaker, more expensive, and just try putting one in your Gatorade.

"I wasn't greedy or anything," says Aaron. "Just got one, stood up straight, did everything right."

"So what? He didn't buy the ID?" says Rudy.

"He just wasn't sure," says Aaron. "And he wanted to take my picture with that stupid little camera on a stick. I was like, 'No way, man.'"

"But you could get the vodka if you let him, right?" says Mars.

Aaron wouldn't take that kind of second-guessing from most people, but with Mars, he shrugs it off. "Not anymore," he says.

"Those things should be illegal," says Rudy.

The irony isn't lost on any of us, except maybe Mars, but it's true. More and more stores around here have these little digital cameras by the register, and they can snap pictures of your face when you buy liquor or cigarettes or whatever. It's not even clear what they do with the pictures, but it's kind of spooky, you know, having your picture taken like that. It's like they're getting the mug shot done in advance.

"Time for Plan B," says Mars.

"You really gonna do that?" says Rudy.

"Hellz yeah," says Mars.

"You are one crazy dude," says Aaron, the smile returning to his face.

"Never denied it," says Mars, smiling back.

Mars starts across the street. He has this idea that he's sure will work. He says he has a cousin who tried it and scored a full case of booze.

It's pretty simple: Go into the store and ask to use the bathroom. Don't do anything suspicious like wear a big jacket that you could stash something in. Just maybe buy a soda and say you really need to go. Then when they let you back there and turn around, look for a side or back door and unlock it. Or maybe wedge something in to keep it from closing all the way. Then you just flush the toilet, say thanks, leave — and head right around back.

So that's Plan B. How many of the one million things that could go wrong can you name? I'm up to around 999,996 when Mars comes back out the front door, carrying a can of Sunkist. He opens it and takes a sip while he's waiting to cross the street. His expression is totally blank, which it probably would be either way.

"Well?" says Aaron, once Mars reaches us.

His face is still unreadable. He likes to do that when he has good news, and I think this is it: He's going to tell us that he left a door open around back and we need to get a move on. My stomach sinks. He takes another sip of his Sunkist.

"Guy's a jerk," he says.

I think I do a pretty good job of hiding my relief. The others rag on him for his plan. Apparently, he's been talking about it all summer. "It'll totally work," says Aaron, imitating Mars's voice. There's some talk of a Plan C, but it doesn't seem to be going anywhere.

"No harm, no foul," I say after a while.

"More like no booze, no beer," says Mars. "Maybe we should try your girlfriend at the 7-Eleven."

That kind of pisses me off. I remember her standing there with her missing tooth and meth tics. But it's true: 7-Eleven does sell beer. "Nah," I say, "you're probably on a most-wanted poster in there by now."

It's a reference to the seventeen cents. He may have seen me talking to the girl through the glass, but there's no way for him to know I covered that. He still thinks he got away with it, and the thought makes him smile: Brantley's most wanted . . . "Oh yeah," he says.

I get up off the bench and Mars takes my place.

"Those are amazingly fake," says Rudy, nodding at Mars's bright white sneakers.

"No way, man," he says, lifting one a few inches off the ground. "They're real Air Jordans, totally old-school."

"Yeah, I'm not sure that school is accredited," says Rudy.

Aaron and I laugh, but Mars doesn't know what that means.

"They're totally real," he repeats. "Old-school." He shifts around and turns his right sneaker over to show us the silhouette of Jordan on the bottom.

"That Jordan looks white," says Rudy, unconvinced.

"Or Chinese," says Aaron.

It's my turn to pile on, but I don't. I don't like making fun of people for what they don't have. A few minutes later, we move on. Our heads are on a swivel, looking for something to do, some way to kill an hour or two before lunch. And that's how the rest of the day goes, just looking for something new. Sometimes we find it, and sometimes we don't. The hours tick by either way, and I get through it all without any real trouble. No harm, no foul.

9

Aaron drops me off in front of my house around four thirty. I have maybe an hour until Mom gets home, and I sort of wonder if I'm going to spend some or all of that cleaning up after the dog. I go in through the kitchen: no dog and no crap there. I find him standing in the middle of the living room. His body is twisted in a C shape so that his back legs are sort of inching forward. His eyes are wide and looking right at me, and his little tail stump is trying to wag. The whole thing, the body language, the eyes, it doesn't seem friendly so much as desperate.

I scan the room. I don't see anything on the floor in here, and just as important, I don't smell anything. "Good boy," I say. People are always saying that to dogs on TV, and I think it's pretty standard.

He gets even more excited as I start toward the back door. He follows me closely, still contorted like a scorpion. Sure enough, the screen door is open the same little sliver it was this morning. "Aw, Johnny," I say. I'm pretty sure it's the first time I've called him by his name, and it is 100 percent out of guilt. "All you had to do was push through."

I'm looking at him and a thought hits me so hard that I know it's true. That's how he wound up chained outside. One mistake, or maybe the guy left him alone for too long and JR couldn't hold it. The kind of guy who'd do that to a dog isn't the kind of guy who'd need much of an excuse. And years later, JR is holding it in again, trying to make up for it or just terrified of what will happen if he can't.

I throw the screen door wide open and hold it there. Johnny's body straightens out and he comes charging toward me. For a moment, I kind of freak out. But he's not coming after me. He just really needs to go. He launches himself out the door like a big black cannonball, clearing the back steps and landing a good three or four feet out into the little yard.

I let the door close behind him and give him his privacy. Then I head to the bathroom to wash the Brantley off me. When I'm done, I go back and open the door. He comes trotting up the steps and into the house like nothing happened. Then I close both doors because it's still really hot out.

"Sorry about that, JR," I say. Now that I'm calling him by name, I'm trying to figure out which version I like best. This one's kind of cool because it's like JD.

I can't quite tell if he's holding a grudge against me or not, so I give him a biscuit. That's got to be his third or fourth of the day. Afterward, he has this look on his face of pure canine contentment. Another thought hits me: He likes it here.

Mom gets home a little later than usual and we have Boston Market microwave dinners, so I know it was a rough day. She's reading the empty box as the microwave blasts away at hers. "These have a lot of salt," she says, frowning.

"Good," I say, after taking a bite of Salisbury steak and swallowing it down with some Coke because it's still pretty hot. I don't mean that it's good it has a lot of salt; I just mean that it's good because I like it and I don't want her to feel bad about dinner.

She looks at my Coke. "And that has a lot of sugar."

"Good!" I say, smiling.

She's about to say something else, but the microwave beeps and cuts her off.

"So what did you do today?" she says, sitting down.

"Not much," I say. I feel like that's true – I feel like that's always true – but I know it's sort of a dodge, so I say, "Just hung out."

"With your friends?" she says.

"Yeah," I say. I want to tell her not to worry about it, that they're not that bad and that I can take care of myself, but I feel like I shouldn't bring that stuff up if she doesn't. Instead, I take a huge bite of the Salisbury steak and work on that for a while. She sees me chewing and doesn't ask me anything else, and I can feel the food burning my mouth.

After dinner, Mom says, "Why don't you take Jon-Jon for a walk?"

I'm like, "First of all, it's Johnny, Johnny Rotten, or JR for short. Second, doesn't he go in the backyard? 'Cause he definitely went there before you got home."

"I think the backyard could use a break," says Mom. "And I think *Johnny* could use a walk."

"I'm not sure we're really there yet, if you know what I mean," I say. "I think he's just, like, using me for food."

But she thinks it's a good idea and hands me the leash.

"Wait, I'm supposed to put this on him?" I say.

"That's how the whole walk thing works," she says.

"Then I definitely don't think we're there yet," I say, but I guess I'm sort of curious. It's not like I have far to go either, since he's been hanging around the table the whole time, hoping for scraps and/or drops.

I take the leash and stand up. He sees the leash, which he definitely recognizes, and he sees me, but he doesn't seem happy about the combination of the two. He starts backing up as I approach. I back him into the corner, like he's a sheep I need to make a sweater out of. The thing is, he's a lot more wolf than sheep. As soon as his butt hits the cabinet, he knows he's cornered, and just like that, some switch flips inside him. His gums come up and there are those big white teeth again: all of them, this time.

He growls. It's not loud, but there's no missing it.

"Whoa!" I say, sort of stumbling back.

"Oh, careful," says Mom.

But it's already over. As soon as I stepped back, he zipped through the gap. He's already in the living room by the time Mom finishes her warning.

"Whoa," I repeat.

"I think he just felt cornered," says Mom. "He was just as scared as you."

She's probably right, but I don't feel like testing her theory any further. I hand the leash back to her and head for the front room. I think I've earned some TV.

10

I look at the time in the corner of the computer screen: It's half past very late, but I can't seem to peel myself away. I've been putting it off, but I finally go to Janie's profile. I tell myself I'm just looking, but I know that's a serious understatement. I've got all night, and the plan is to pore through it: to scroll through all of the status updates and wall posts since I left; to click through her new pictures and the pictures of the people in them. I'm looking for signs of some other guy, some dude with his arm around her at a party or leaving messages for her or, well, any of the things that I used to do, basically. It's a lot of work and maybe a little insane, but I haven't been sleeping much anyway.

It's a very short trip. I'm sitting there waiting for her page to load, wondering what's up with my connection, when I realize that it has loaded. I can only get the partial view, the "limited profile." I didn't see that coming. Did she cut me off? It's the first thing I think. Someone must've told her I'm back, or she found out somehow, and she put up the deflector shields. It's a total kick in the crotch, and for a while, I just sit there staring at the few things on the screen: the same profile pic she always uses; her hometown, same as mine; and her birthday with no year. Then I spend a few seconds confirming that nothing is clickable, even though I was already fairly sure of that.

Finally, my pride kicks in and I start looking for other explanations. Maybe she got another message from the Creeper. There was this guy who started sending her weird messages and commenting on her pictures and stuff like that last winter. He's really old, maybe even retired, and it sort of freaked her out. He lives a few states away, but I think she was a little worried that he would hop in his unmarked pervert van and make the trip. I was kind of worried, too, but I was also hoping for the chance to beat him into a little pile of creep dust.

So maybe he's back. Or maybe there's another one. The world is full of creepy dudes, I tell myself — and then I realize that the only guy I know for sure is obsessing over Janie's profile tonight is me.

I click over to my page. I sort of feel like hiding it, too, just out of pride, but I realize that it would affect approximately no one. The page is a total ghost town. I haven't posted anything in months.

I'm not sure how this computer can make me feel any worse tonight, but I figure I'll give it a try. I Google "rescue dogs." That does the trick. I'm sort of looking for clues about why ours acts the way he does, but I have to click away after a few minutes. It's the pictures — what they were rescued from. The dogs are filthy or beat-up, lying in mud or covered in ticks. One of them has a broken leg. It's not, like, in a clean white cast; it's bent, broken, and dirty. The caption says "Bonnie, lab. mix, approx. 1 year old."

I guess I hadn't really thought about that part: how bad it has to be before a dog gets rescued. On the one hand, it makes me sad, but on the other hand — well, that hand is a fist. There's a picture of this guy who was keeping pit bulls in his basement. It's right after the dogs got taken away, and he's smiling like it's nothing, like a kid who broke a plate. I feel like I did when Janie told me about the Creeper: that same anger toward someone you don't really know, but you also sort of do know.

The computer screen is still on when I get up on Tuesday. The screen saver is dancing around and when I hit the space bar, a page about this year's "NFL Impact Rookies" appears. I don't even remember looking at that, and I feel really groggy. I was up so late that this morning just feels like more of the same day.

I want to go back to sleep, but it's already close to eleven and Rudy is coming over soon to see JR. That makes me think of the pictures from last night. It's hard to think of him that way, beat-up and filthy. It makes me angry again, but I feel like I've been angry for months, and I need to chill out.

Anyway, I head straight to the kitchen to get some cereal, because you can't properly chill out on an empty stomach. Fifteen minutes later, I'm one bowl of Crunch Berries in and considering a shower when Rudy knocks on the door. I'm still half-asleep, so the first thing I say is really dumb: "Hey, man. I was about to take a shower."

He shakes his head and says, "Well, I'm not joining you, if that's what you mean."

And then I'm just backpedaling and digging myself deeper. "No, no, I mean, I didn't. I'm glad I didn't. I hate it when you're in the shower and, like, hear something, you know? Always freaks me out."

"O-o-o-kay then," he says, stepping inside.

"Sorry, man," I say. "Up late."

"Yeah," he says. "Whole summer without porn. Must've been tough."

"Yeah," I say. "It was going to be a cold shower."

And then he laughs and I do, too.

"Whoa," he says. "Is that him?"

I look back over my shoulder. Johnny is standing by the doorway to the living room, hoping for a biscuit. "Nah," I say. "That's some other dog."

"Can I pet 'im?" says Rudy, but he takes a step forward and Johnny takes a step back, and that basically answers that question.

"I don't know, man. I think he had it pretty rough. My mom says he's, like, not so-down with men, 'cause his last owner was a dude. And a jerk."

"Was he having him fight and stuff?" says Rudy.

"I don't think so," I say. "Mom says he was just kept outside, chained to a tree. And maybe beaten."

"That all?"

"Yeah, right."

"Geez, look at his head," says Rudy. "It's like a . . . I don't even know. Look at his mouth!"

Johnny is standing half on the kitchen tile and half off. I think he knows we're talking about him. I turn back to Rudy. "Watch this," I say, and head over to the biscuit jar.

Johnny is all kinds of conflicted, torn between sheer love of biscuits and total distrust of dudes. He doesn't come quite as close with both of us there, but that just makes the leaping chomp more impressive.

"Awesome!" says Rudy. "It's like those sharks."

"That's what I thought!"

As Air Jaws finishes gulping down the biscuit and vacuums the crumbs off the floor, I give him a close look. His fur is pretty much smooth and shiny — I know Mom has been giving him this special dry food — but there's this one patch above his left hind leg. It's on the border between his black hip and his brown leg, and the fur there is a little thinner and doesn't really lie flat. I wonder how he got that: a scar, maybe, or ticks.

"I'd sort of like to find the guy," I say.

"I think that'd be a bad idea," says Rudy.

"What do you think, namewise: Johnny or JR? I can't call him Johnny Rotten all the time."

"I think maybe JR," says Rudy. "Like JD."

"I thought that, too," I say. Rudy's been my friend for so long that we think alike sometimes. Or maybe that's why we became friends. It works out the same either way.

"Hey, JR," he says.

JR looks over, and he definitely knows that's him. His ears perk up a little, and I'm pretty sure he's thinking: Is this new person also a potential food source? He must decide he's not, because he wheels around and heads for his spot in the corner of the living room. Mom moved his water dish there, so it's officially his place now.

"Cool," says Rudy. "You see his ears move?"

"Yeah," I say.

"It's kind of a downer to see a big dog like that so freaked out."

"Yeah," I say. "I'm sort of thinking maybe he won't always be."

"Well, let me know," he says. "Because that dog would be a chick *magnet*."

"You think?" I say. The thought had definitely crossed my mind. "Don't they like the little dogs? Like purse sized and rat looking?"

"That's just what they get for themselves," he says. "Really, they like the big dogs."

"That's awesome," I say.

"Big Dog!" Rudy calls out toward the living room, and maybe because he knows what it means or maybe because he still isn't familiar with Rudy's voice, we get one loud bark back.

"HAARRFF!"

11

We spend a couple of hours on the PlayStation. I'm really out of practice, and Rudy pretty much kills me continuously. One of the few times I win is because he gets a text message at exactly the wrong moment, and I perforate him with the nail gun while he's checking it.

Turns out, the text is from Aaron. They're going to Wendy's. Rudy texts back, saying to pick us up here, but I can't help noticing that I never get a text. Twenty minutes later, the car pulls up. Rudy and Mars both live within walking distance, and sometimes they'll just show up, but Aaron always arrives this way. He never pulls into the driveway, just rolls to a stop along the side of the road, like it's a bank heist. That's fine because he almost never gets out of the car. Except today, he and Mars both do. I see both front doors open as Rudy and I are heading toward the car.

"What's up?" I call out.

"Wanna see the dog," calls Mars. He waits for Aaron to come around the front of the car, and then they start across the yard together.

"Nah," I start. I look over to Rudy to back me up, but he's kind of poker faced, and I wonder if he mentioned something about it in his message. "I don't think you should."

"What the hell," says Mars. "Why not?"

He stops six feet in front of me. I stop, too.

"He's new," I say. "Kind of weird around people."

Mars points to Rudy and me with his right hand, palm up, meaning: You're people, aren't you? Mars and Aaron are in front of me and Rudy is a few steps behind. I feel a little boxed in.

"Maybe, like, Thursday," I say. I don't really mean that. I'm just trying to put him off because I think one new dude is enough for today. And Aaron is always under control, but I don't really trust Mars to be cool around the dog.

Mars says something under his breath. I can't make it out, but Aaron laughs and shakes his head. It's some inside joke, possibly about me. They turn and head back to the car, and I wonder if I just made a big mistake.

Wendy's is out by the interstate, and the ride over is pretty quiet. But once we all have our food spread out on one of the two outside tables, they start interrogating me about where I was over the summer. I know immediately that I'm not going to have the energy to do this right, and I wonder if they know that too, like this was all planned out. I feel tired and grungy. I should've showered; at least it would've woken me up some.

"Dude, man, seriously," says Aaron. "Where were you?"

"You mean what town?" I say, because I've told them four dozen times that I was at my aunt's place.

"I mean, what center?" says Aaron.

"Yeah," says Mars. "Was it the big one up in Milford? I hear it's rough."

"It wasn't any of them, and it wasn't rough," I say. "Just really boring."

"Seriously," says Aaron. "I think you need to give that a rest. I don't even know why you started it. Or, OK, maybe you were embarrassed or whatever, and you said that to some other people and you felt like you had to keep your story straight. I understand that. But it's us, dude. You need to drop it."

"Seriously," repeats Mars. "It's not like it's not kind of cool anyway. And what? We're gonna *judge* you or something? Look at us!"

I can't help but look around. Mars is wearing an orange T-shirt with a jack-o'-lantern face on the front and a faded brown stain running from eye to mouth. It's a Halloween shirt he probably got for Christmas, 60 percent off by then. Aaron is wearing his Avenged Sevenfold concert T-shirt, which probably cost a fortune. And Rudy is still wearing the skeleton shirt from yesterday, purchased online with an M&S Realty credit card. *M&S* stands for Mark and Sandy, his parents, and he keeps the charges small and scattered. File under miscellaneous expenses.

Rudy hasn't said anything yet, and I'm thinking that he's on my side. And so of course he catches me completely off guard.

"What's her name?" he says. "Your aunt."

"It's, uh, it's Judy," I say, but that little hesitation goes off like thunder. The table is quiet for a second. I can't believe I did that.

"What a load of crap!" says Mars.

"What?" I say. "Her name is Judy."

No one's buying it, and I look over at Rudy. I wonder why he did it.

12

I usually go to bed around midnight, and sometimes much later, but I barely make it to eleven on Tuesday. I'm completely wiped out. Plus, I take some Benadryl because I'm "suffering" from "allergies," and that stuff always knocks me out. I sleep like a rock. I wake up early and decide I might as well get an early start on doing nothing. It's good practice anyway, since I'll have to start getting up for school again in like five days. Not looking forward to that.

Mom is running late and surprised to see me before she leaves. She's standing in the kitchen, dressed super sharp and carrying an enormous travel mug of coffee, even though she travels less than a mile to the office.

"You look like a politician," I say, grabbing the cereal box and getting started on breakfast.

"That's me," she says. "You look like a sleepy, rumpled teenager."

"That's me," I say. I guess we've got each other figured out.

"What's the occasion?" she asks.

"Gotta milk the chickens and feed the cows," I say.

"Well, how about walking the dog while you're at it?"

I have to admit, it fits right in on my list of imaginary farm chores, but I don't think so. "Nah," I say. "Kind of hoping to get through the day without getting mauled."

"I'll put the leash on for you," she says.

"He'll let you?" I say.

"Sure, I've done it before."

"Dude," I call over my shoulder into the living room. I want to say, "Bros before hos," but it's my mom, so that's pretty much out of the question. I think about it for a second. "Brothas before mothas!" I shout.

We both laugh at that, and then I can't figure out how to get back to no from there. Mom barely waits for my response anyway. She puts down her travel mug, picks up the leash, and heads into the living room. I listen for a growl or anything like that, but all I hear is the sound of metal clicking on metal and then both of them heading back to the kitchen.

"Out!" Mom announces once they arrive.

"I'm not done," I say, pointing to my cereal.

"It will be there when you get back," she says.

It will be milk paste when I get back, but she's made up her mind, and I guess I'm curious to see if this will actually work.

"Out!" she repeats, except this time she's talking to the dog. He's walking more or less normally on the end of a blue nylon leash. She opens the door in front of her, and they both head out into the yard. I follow after them, bringing her travel mug and closing the door behind me. It's not as hot today, and the sun is half hidden behind some low clouds.

I hand Mom the mug and she hands me the leash. JR's body language changes immediately. His head shoots back and forth between us, registering the bait and switch. His shoulders slump and his brown legs fold halfway to the ground. His eyes flash with confusion and something worse, maybe betrayal.

"Geez," I say. It's hard not to take it personally.

"He'll be fine once you get going," says Mom, already walking toward the car.

"Was he like this the first time you walked him?" I say.

"Not exactly," she calls back. "But then, I'd showered."

The car pulls out and it's just the two of us: an unwashed dude and a slouching dog. I don't trust him, and he doesn't trust me, but we can't stay there forever. "Come on, man," I say. "You were walking fine for her. What, 'cause she has a suit?"

He's not listening to me as much as watching me talk. His ears are back in a way that looks hostile. "Come on, man," I repeat. A car goes by, and then another. Finally, I give the leash a little tug. It feels like pulling the pin out of a grenade. I'm thinking, Yep, this is the part where he jumps up and bites my neck off.

Instead, he takes a step. It's a small one, but it's not toward my neck. I give the leash another little tug, and he takes another little step. He's still crouched down, and his legs are still bent halfway between sitting and standing, but those were definitely steps. I give the leash another tug.

"I can do this for as long as my throat remains in my body," I say. "So you're going to have to go ahead and bite my head off now or get moving."

His ears come forward. I think that means he's listening.

"Big Dog," I say.

I start walking, just little steps.

He does, too.

I lengthen out my strides.

He straightens out his legs.

Holy crap, we're walking.

He's at the absolute maximum distance from me that the leash will allow, but he's no longer even looking at me. He's looking around. Our neighbors' door opens and closes and he checks it out. A bird lands on the grass ten yards away and he watches it. It takes off again and he follows it the whole way, his head tracking it up and back.

"That's right," I say to the bird. "You better run!"

He watches me say that too, but I'm just another sight now, and a second later he's looking at something else. He loves this stuff, and by the time we reach the edge of the backyard, it's like he's almost forgotten that I'm there.

Once we reach the bike path, his head is all over the place, sniffing the ground one moment and peering into the bushes the next. I'd never spent enough time around a dog before to realize this, but they have a lot of the same expressions as people. Before, when I saw one on TV or whatever, I used to think: That's funny, it almost looks like he's sad or happy or whatever. Now I'm look-ing down at JR, and I realize he really is smiling, a big, drooly dog smile. He's happy just to be outside and moving. I guess after years of being chained to a tree and covered in ticks you can't quite reach, that's about as good as it gets.

"This isn't so bad, huh, boy?" I say.

He looks back at me. I sort of expect the smile to drop off his face, but it doesn't. I know he's not smiling at me — that he's probably doing it despite me — but I'm glad he keeps doing it. The bent tree is coming up, and I start to angle us over toward that side of the trail so I can give it my standard slap. "This is my tree, JR," I say.

He looks back at me, sniffs the tree once, and lifts his leg.

"That is just wrong!" I say, but I'm laughing.

We take our time and make it almost all the way to the bridge before turning around. Afterward, I manage to get the leash off him without too much trouble, but he definitely gets weird again once we're back inside, and he heads straight to his corner in the living room. So it's not like all of a sudden we completely understand each other, but it was a good walk. I think we're both surprised.

I spot my phone on the kitchen table, next to my liquefied cereal. No calls, no texts, nothing. As I'm checking, I realize something stinks in here. I take a few deep whiffs and, sure enough, it's me. I'm rank. I get some clean clothes and head to the bathroom to shower. Might as well do this right. I've got something to do later, and I don't want to show up looking like the Swamp Thing.

Hey, Johnny didn't bite my head off today. Maybe Janie won't, either.

13

I end up waiting around for Mom to get home, hoping she'll let me take the car. She doesn't. I mean, she does get home, but she doesn't let me take the car.

"Baby bird," she says, deepening the wound, "you don't have your license yet."

Like I could possibly forget that.

"I've got my permit!"

"Yes, but you need a licensed driver with you," she says.

I hate that part.

"And I'm tired," she adds.

I literally, physically cringe. Showing up at Janie's for the first time in months with my mom in the passenger seat . . . It's almost too horrible to imagine. She does look tired, though. This morning, her suit looked pressed. Now it looks de-pressed.

"Fine," I say. "I'll take my bike."

"Be back before dark," she says, like I hoped she would.

"Nope, going to get hit in the dark," I say. "Pretty dangerous out there on the side of the road at night."

Now I'm thinking that she's fallen into my trap and she will let me take the car after all.

"Well, then, you can't go at all," she says.

D'oh!

Now I can resort to pleading or call her bluff.

"Fine," I say, and head for the door.

"Be back before dark," she says to my back.

I don't argue anymore. The truth is, I'll probably be back in about half an hour. It's like a fifteen-minute ride, and there's a pretty good chance Janie won't want anything to do with me. I start to imagine worst-case scenarios: the door slammed in my face and things like that.

I get going and power up the first big hill of the ride without too much trouble. I reach the top and shift gears for the coast down. I'm sweating now, but the wind on the ride down cools me off a little. I shift gears again for the straightaway and try to flatten out my wind-tunnel hair as I ride. I'm not wearing a bike helmet because that is precisely the sort of midlevel semibadass I am.

I barely make it up the third hill. Three hills will do that to you, but worse than the cramp in my side is that fact that it feels really lame to be biking to her house. It wasn't as bad last year, when I was still a sophomore and it seemed like I'd have my license any day. We used to joke about it: "In like Schwinn!" Now I'm a few days away from being a junior, and no closer to that license. Just watch: I'm going to get there, lean my bike against the tree out front, and there's going to be a frickin' Porsche in the driveway, owned by her new boyfriend, Dale Earnhardt Jr.

I try to shake the thought out of my head. It is so two hills ago. And who knows, she could be happy to see me. Maybe she missed me. . . . Maybe her parents are out. . . . Maybe it will be just like it was before. . . . Now I'm pedaling faster again, faster and faster. It's been a lonely summer.

By the time I arrive, I'm back to looking like the Swamp Thing. On the plus side, no Porsche. There are two cars in the driveway: her parents' SUV and the little hybrid that I realize is probably hers now. I let my bike drop in the grass, like the non-helmet wearer I am, and start toward the door before I can change my mind.

I walk slowly, not because I'm nervous, or at least not entirely. It's turned into a fairly cool evening, there's a nice breeze, and now that I'm off the bike, I need to, well, I need to dry. As it turns out, I have plenty of time. I reach the door, take a deep breath, and knock twice.

Nothing.

Twice more.

Nothing.

Come on, people. Your lights are on. Your cars are in the driveway. I'm wondering if they saw me pull up, if they know it's me. I go to push my hand through my hair, and I can feel it crunch. It's the hair gel. I found a year-old sample tube of L.A. Looks in the back of the medicine cabinet today and used the whole thing. The sweat must have reactivated it, and now my hair has dried in the upright-and-locked position.

The door opens. It's Janie's father, Adrian. That may sound like a girl's name, but it's a guy's name in Romania, where all six-feet-four of him is from. He's terrifying, and I'm pretty sure he has always hated me. It was during one rare thaw that he cracked a smile and said, "Call me Adrian." Now I'm standing there, my hand stuck halfway through my hair, and I'm not sure what to call him.

"Hi, Mr. Pera," I say, playing it safe and pulling my hand free.

"Hello," he says in his Count Dracula accent.

"Is, uh, Janie home?" My voice comes out smaller than I want, but at least it's a coherent sentence.

"No," he says.

He hesitates, trying to think of something to add. He's not a talkative guy at all, but even for him, a one-word dismissal of a guy who looks like he just ran 26.2 miles to get here is a little harsh.

"Your hair," he says. "It has a problem."

"Yeah, I know," I say. I'm pretty sure it's standing straight up. This is not the "absolute styling performance" I was promised.

"Well, she is not here," he says, finding his rhythm. "I will tell her you stopped by. Good night."

He closes the door in my face. I'm not sure that's his intention, but that's where my face is, so that's the effect closing the door has. I stand there for a few seconds, kind of reeling. It's like, Nice to see you, too, *Adrian*. Then I walk back to my stupid bike. I resist the urge to look in every window as I pass, but I allow myself a quick look up at her bedroom.

The light is on, but the blinds are closed. Don't jump to conclusions, I tell myself. It doesn't mean she's home. She might just have forgotten to turn the light off when Junior picked her up in the Porsche.

14

I sleep in Thursday morning, because why not? It's an overcast gray day and it took me forever to get to sleep again. I kept thinking the same thing, over and over again: Why didn't I just call? I thought biking over made sense yesterday. It seemed like the kind of industrial-strength relationship repair work that needed to be done in person. Plus, I tried to call a few times this summer and nothing. But if she knew I was back, she'd probably answer. She's going to see me at school in a few days. Anyway, I don't think I got to sleep before three or four.

Mom is gone by the time I get up, but I'm pretty sure JR will let me put the leash on him now. I'm actually looking forward to it – another mile or so of scaring the crap out of this town's squirrels – but I don't see him downstairs. It's not until I go to get the milk out of the fridge that I see the note: *Let dog in.* I get the marker and write *Who let the dog out?* underneath. I figure I'll do it after I eat, but midway through the bowl, I hear something going on out back.

It's just one bark and a shout, but right away I have a really bad feeling. I recognize the voice. I'm up, out of my chair, and through the back door in about four seconds. Sure enough, there's Mars.

He's standing right outside the fence, and I'm about to ask him what the noise is about. But then I see his right hand. He's holding it in close to his body, and there's blood on it. I look over and see JR hunkered down against the back corner of the fence.

Oh no. No, no, no.

Mars looks up and sees me standing there. "He bit me," he says. "He bit me!"

"What're you doing here?" I say, trying to maybe turn this back on him.

"You said I could see him today," he says, and I guess that's technically true.

"I didn't really mean . . . right now," I say, but it comes out sounding more like a question.

I know right away that this is bad. The blood is deep red and dangerous looking, and as I'm watching, a fat drop falls from the tip of his middle finger right into the crisscrossed laces of one of his fake Jordans. This is bad, bad, bad. Not many people lose their lives to dog bites these days. But lots of dogs do.

PART·II

IN THE DOGHOUSE

15

I'm standing at the top of the three steps that lead into the back-yard. I look at Mars's face and then down at his hand again. It's been a while since I've seen him like this, hurt and bleeding. "Well, you better come in and get that cleaned up," I say, pushing the screen door open a little wider to show what I mean.

Mars looks over at JR, but the dog still hasn't moved from the patch of dirt in the corner of the fence. "He's not going to chase you," I say.

Mars edges up to one of the wooden fence posts and puts his good hand on it, his eyes on JR the whole time. He sort of bends his knees, and I realize he's going to hop the fence.

"Dude, there's a gate right there," I say.

"Oh yeah," he says.

He walks over and flips the latch up. He takes one more quick look back to confirm that he's in the clear and steps into the yard and straight toward the back steps.

"Watch your step, there's —"

"I know," he says, cutting me off. "The grass is full of dog crap."

Something about that statement seems wrong. Something

about this whole thing seems wrong, but my mind is buzzing and I can't quite place it.

"What did you do?" I say.

"I just . . ." he starts, but then he seems to think better of it.

"Yeah, you just what?" I say.

He looks at me but avoids my eyes. "I got bit, all right?"

There's something he's not telling me, something maybe I already know, but I don't want to push things right now. I need to be cool about this, be extra nice.

"All right, all right," I say, holding the door wide for him.

We have a pretty good stash of bandages and Bactine and all that stuff in the bathroom. I had more than my share of skateboard wipeouts and tree-climbing free falls when I was a kid, and Mom has kept the medicine cabinet stocked up ever since.

"Hold it over the sink," I say, turning on the water.

He's holding his hand like a claw, the fingers half curled, and he's already bled on the floors of three different rooms, including this one. As he moves it another fat drop falls and disappears in the swirl of running water.

"OK," I say, once I have the temperature about right.

He puts his hand under the faucet; the water turns red, then pink, then almost clear. I grab a wad of toilet paper and hand it to him.

"Let me see."

He pulls the wet clump of paper away and for a second I see it clearly: two holes in the skin on the back of his hand, with some smaller red marks leading up to them. The holes are a little rough around the edges; *tears* might be a better word. That must be where the big canine teeth went in. And then, as I watch them, fresh blood pushes its way to the surface: two slick drops, expanding like tiny red balloons. Mars puts the balled-up paper back on his hand and I push through the cabinet, looking for something to cover that up with. Gauze, maybe, or two big bandages? I decide to go with all of the above.

"First things first," I say, taking the small plastic bottle of antiseptic out.

"What's that?" he says.

"You never used Bactine?" I say. That seems weird to me. Mars was at least as accident prone as I was. What did his parents put on his cuts and scrapes? I think about his parents. Cheap whiskey, probably.

"Nope," he says.

"It cleans things up," I say. "Prevents infection."

"Oh crap!" he says, stiffening up. "What if I get rabies?"

"You're not going to get rabies," I say, and I squirt the Bactine on his hand.

"Aaaah!" he says, but he's being a baby because Bactine doesn't even sting that much.

"I'm just cleaning it up, man," I say, handing him a fresh handful of paper.

I bandage him up and he leaves through the front door.

"Want to borrow an umbrella?" I say, one last attempt to make nice.

We both look up at the clouds. They're definitely darker now than the last time we saw them, not fifteen minutes ago.

"Nah," he says. "Just going straight home. I'll make it."

As he walks away, all the gauze and tape make him look like a burn victim. I should've only used two bandages, but I was trying to be extra helpful. Stupid, I think, but the damage has already been done. Boy, has it. Now he's heading home to whichever one of his parents is currently unemployed — one of them always seems to be — looking like he was well and truly mauled.

Then I go out back to get Johnny. I open the door to the backyard and say, "Well, Air Jaws, you've done it this time."

He looks up at me, but he still hasn't moved from his corner. Calling him doesn't work, so I head out there to get him. I keep my eyes glued to the tall grass, looking for land mines, but apart from that, I don't really have a plan. I should have brought his leash, or maybe a biscuit. I feel a small raindrop hit my neck. A second later, another one lands on my wrist.

"Come on in before you get rained on," I say. "No one likes that wet dog smell."

I slow down as I get closer because I remember that JR doesn't like to be cornered. I guess I'm remembering all that blood, too. I reach the edge of the bare spot near the post, and that's where I see it. Just inches in front of where JR is crouched, there's a fresh footprint in the dirt. In the middle of it, I can just make out the head, arm, and shoulders of a little man, a ball in his tiny hand: Air Jordan.

"That scumbag," I say.

JR cocks his head at the sound of my voice. He's the nearest one to me, and it's definitely not his finest moment, but I don't mean him. I mean the guy I just saw a few feet and one easily hoppable fence from where I'm standing. The scumbag I'm talking about is the one who jumped the fence and cornered my dog.

Through the screen door, I hear the phone start ringing. It mixes with the sound of the rain beginning to fall all around us.

"That's not going to be good," I say.

JR looks right at me. His wet brown eyes look almost black in the dim light. This time, I am talking to him.

16

It's much easier to convince JR to come inside after it starts raining. The phone stops ringing before I get to it, but it starts up again before I can check the voice mail. It's my mom, and she's upset.

"What happened?" she says, but from the tone of her voice I can tell she knows at least the basics.

"Mars got bit," I say. "Johnny bit him."

"Is he OK?"

"Yeah, he's fine," I say. "He's just a little spooked or something. He didn't want to come inside."

"No, no, Dominic," she says. She always calls Mars by his real name. "Is he OK? Could you tell?"

"Yeah, yeah, he's fine. He's got, like, some holes in his hand. Just little ones. I could've used bandages, but I used gauze, just because. He's fine."

"That's not what his mom says," she says. That makes me a little mad. It's like, I am your son, Mom. It's OK to believe me.

"She's a frickin' drunk. What did she say?"

"Oh, don't say that."

"It's true."

"Still."

"OK, whatever. What did she say?"

"They're taking him to the hospital," she says. She pauses and then adds, "I'm not sure they really have insurance."

I hardly know where to start with that. This is so ridiculous. First of all, it wasn't that bad. It's not like anything was broken or he was going to need stitches for two little holes the size of BBs. We've definitely all had worse. I do a quick memory check of our run-ins with broken glass and barbed wire and bike or board wipeouts, and every one of them makes me madder.

"Mars is full of it," I say, finally. I think that sums it up pretty well. "What're they going to do, send us the bill or something?"

"Yes," says Mom, "they are."

"Well, make them send it directly. Tell them you need to see the real bill, otherwise they'll just make it up."

"Oh, Jimmer, we'll be lucky if we get off that easy."

"What do you mean?" I say. "Wait, what do you mean?"

I look over at JR, who has already hunkered down in his normal spot. Mom still hasn't answered me.

"What's going to happen?"

"Let's not think about that now, OK?" she says. "I'll just pay their bill and you be nice to Dominic and hopefully that will be that."

"That lowlife!"

"That doesn't help," she says. "You send him an e-mail or a text message or a Skype thingy or whatever it is he uses later and ask him how he is."

"I'll punch him in the head and ask him how he is," I say, but I sort of know she's right. She does, too, so she waits me out for a few seconds.

"I'll text him later," I say.

"OK," she says.

"OK," I say, and then I remember that I haven't even told her what happened. Sometimes I think I just expect her to know everything because she's my mom, but there's no way she could know this.

"But, but, but," I start, in a huge hurry all of a sudden, "it wasn't even his fault — JR's, I mean — because Mars cornered him —"

"What do you —"

"Yeah, he hopped the fence and Johnny must've backed away and he backed him up and probably stuck his hand right in his face to pet him — and you know how Johnny doesn't like any of that, and —"

"Did you see this?" Mom says.

"No," I say. "But there was, um, there was a footprint, his footprint, like right there, and he was definitely in the yard. So it's not Johnny's fault, right? I mean, Mars can't just jump the fence and corner a dog and stick —"

"There's a footprint?" Mom says.

I look out the window and see the big drops thumping against the glass and splashing off the sill.

"Not anymore," I say.

"And you didn't see him?"

"But I know . . ."

"I know, baby bird."

Neither of us says anything for a little while. Finally, Mom says, "I have to get back to work. Are you OK?"

As if a dog bite was the kind of thing that could ricochet.

"Yeah, I'm fine."

I feel my cell vibrate in my pocket, just once, so it's a text.

"OK, bye," I say.

"I'll be home later."

I hang up one phone and pull out the other. The text is from Rudy: **Mars got bit??? What??? He's at hospital!!!!!**

That didn't take long, I think. And I know exactly how it happened: Mars to Aaron to Rudy and back to me. I immediately start typing my reply, but I scrap it. For some reason, I feel like I have to be really careful what I say right now, even to my friends. Especially to my friends.

JR gets up and walks across the room. I watch him lean down over his water dish and wash the Mars out of his mouth.

"Get it all out," I say. "Get it all out, boy."

17

The rain stops around two o'clock, and the sun's out by three. By three thirty, I'm ready to get the heck out of the house. I get the leash and walk over toward JR. He's in his spot and sort of pre-cornered, so I'm thinking: Don't push it, dude. If he doesn't want the leash on, don't try to put it on.

Turns out, he does want the leash on. I click it into place with no trouble at all, and we head straight out the door.

"Out the do'!" I say, pushing it open. JR shakes his head as he steps out, his ears flapping back and forth and his collar jangling.

It's late summer, after a good, hard rain. The sun is getting to work drying things out, and it's like the whole town has been power washed, just clean and green as far as the eye can see. It feels like a fresh start. I know it's not, and that no amount of rain can magically un-bite someone, but that's what I want it to feel like, so I let it. Still, I take JR around back and head toward the bike path, because I don't want anyone else jamming a hand in his face trying to pet him.

Or if they do, I want it to be somewhere I can easily dispose of the body.

Kidding. Sort of.

Anyway, the grass is wet and spongy and Johnny loves it. He stops to drink from a puddle, but I'm like, "Dude, that's nasty."

I give his leash a little tug, and he's just as happy to get moving again. I sort of wonder if he's doing the same thing I am: pretending everything is totally fine. The other options are that he's dumb as a post or just super Zen. I actually think it might be some of each. I think that might be what it's like to be a dog.

Anyway, by the time we hit the trail, he's thinking his dog thoughts and his head is on a swivel, looking for birds and squirrels and sniffing everything. I'm thinking my human ones. Mainly, they're about Mars. I honestly do feel a little bad that he got bit. You know, no matter whose fault it was and how much it's going to cost Mom or maybe JR, it still sucks to get your hand chomped like that.

Now it's a problem for everyone, though, and that's mostly what I'm thinking about. Mars and I have known each other for a long time, and we used to be good friends. Rudy, too. It's like Rudy and I were best friends and Mars was our other friend. Mom used to call us the Mud Brothers, because we were usually covered in dirt and grass stains.

We were close in that little-kid way. Mars was always kind of crazy, but back then that mostly meant that, for example, he'd eat absolutely anything. Rudy and I thought it was funny, and Mars definitely enjoyed the attention. And it wasn't just eating things; it was climbing them or saying them or being the first to try a board slide on a new railing.

But right around the time that the willingness to eat an earthworm stopped being cool and just became abnormal, Aaron moved to town. He was a big, blue-eyed kid — the only one of the four of us with anything other than brown — and he showed up on the first day of fifth grade like a little Viking come to take our stuff and pummel us at dodgeball. He thought Mars was hilarious from the start — all those old stunts were new to him. He needed a sidekick, and that's who he picked.

That was the end of the Mud Brothers. Rudy and I still saw Mars all the time, but he was almost always with Aaron, and when he wasn't, it was like he was waiting for him. Because I think Aaron makes him feel important. And I think, toward the end there, Rudy and I probably made him feel the opposite. Like, Mars would be the one scraped up from a skateboard crash or sick from something he ate, and we'd be the ones laughing about it.

And that foundation has had plenty of time to set in place by now. That foundation is 100 percent dry. I used to be able to talk Mars into or out of anything. Now I need to find a way to do it again. Because there's one other thing I know: Mom is scared about this. I could hear it in her voice on the phone today. She's afraid, and it isn't about the hospital bill. She even said so. Mars and his mom could do a lot worse than that to us now. To us, but mostly to JR.

There's an older couple coming down the trail toward us. I know who they are, but I forget their name. Maybe Fogel? Fogg? Fogelfogg? Something with an *F* anyway.

"Be cool, boy," I say.

I walk us over to the opposite side of the path, but the Fs see us and start angling in our direction.

"What a handsome dog!" says Mrs. F.

"That's a Rottweiler, isn't it?" says Mr. F.

"What's his name?" says Mrs. F.

"Yeah," I say, sort of putting my body between JR and them. "His name is Johnny."

That seems like enough. Based on the matching light blue Windbreakers, the Fs don't seem so punk rock to me.

"Hi, Johnny!" says Mrs. F.

JR raises his gummy black lips and shows his teeth. He's ignoring Mrs. F. and looking straight at her husband. There's no doubt about it; he's snarling at this old man. They're looking at him all over, kind of ogling him, to be honest, and I'm not sure they've noticed yet.

"Johnny!" I say, and give his leash a sharp tug.

He looks back at me and his lips drop back over his teeth.

"Good dog!" says Mr. F. And then, "Does he bite?"

What he means is: Can we pet him? He definitely didn't see the snarl, and now they're starting to lean in toward him. JR is still staring at Mr. F. I see his mouth twitch, like maybe he's going to show some teeth again or start barking. I give his leash another tug.

"He's been known to," I say. I say it like maybe I'm joking, but it stops them from leaning in any closer, and I'm glad for that.

"Really?" says Mrs. F. She has half a smile on her face, not sure what to think.

"Nah," I say. It's a total lie, but that information is on a need-to-know basis. Johnny's eyes are darting from Mr. F. to me and his back legs start bending a little, like maybe he's going to sit down. Mrs. F. starts reaching for him again, but he's still staring at her husband and doesn't seem to notice.

"He's a little" — I can't think of the word, and I need it fast — "skittish, is all."

She stops and looks up at me.

"Why's that, now?" she says. The half smile turns into half a frown and you can tell she thinks that maybe it's because of me. Whatever, I've got her answer.

"He's a rescue," I say.

"Oh," she says.

"Oh," says her husband.

They both look at him again, but this time they really see him: his eyes wide open, afraid or angry or both, his legs bending back away from them. Mrs. F. takes a step back.

"That's awful," she says, "that someone would treat a nice dog like that."

"What did they do to him? Was he a fighting dog?" says Mr. F. "Sort of looks like a fighting dog."

"Nah," I say. "Chained him up, beat him."

I don't know if that second part is true, but I point to the messed-up patch of fur.

"Ticks," I say.

"Shameful," says Mrs. F.

"Did anything happen to that jerk?" says Mr. F.

"No," I say, "but we're going to look for him now."

They think that's pretty funny and step aside.

"Well, we hope you find him!" says Mrs. F.

Twenty yards later, JR is back to sniffing the ground and looking for squirrels.

"Good-bye, Johnny!" Mrs. F calls out behind us.

He lifts his head and looks back.

"I'm taking a real chance being out here with public enemy number one," I say to him.

His eyes flick up at me.

"But you did good," I say. "Yeah, met three people today and only bit one. Think you may have a Nobel Peace Prize coming your way. Or a Nobel Beast Prize any —"

And then something moves in the bushes, and it's like nothing else exists in his world. Again I'm thinking: dumb as a post or super Zen? I give him a little extra leash, and he charges forward and scares the heck out of some sort of small bird, not a sparrow, but about that size. He watches it fly away and then goes back to sniffing the damp ground.

"What are you even going to smell after all that rain?" I say to him. He doesn't look up this time. He's caught scent of something. Shows what I know.

When we get home, JR goes to his corner and I go to the front room and take out my phone.

hey man! hope the hand is ok! sorry about that. dog is still a little weird w/ people — but hey at least he's got good taste :o srsly, sorry. let me know u r ok!

I look it over again and hit send. I think it's pretty good. I said sorry twice, made a lame joke, and didn't use any capital letters because Mars never does. Now I want a quick text back: **am fine, thx 4 help** or **no prob. my fault** would be ideal, but I'll settle for **im ok screw u.** Instead, I get nothing. The phone just sits there. I turn on the TV, and I just sit there, too.

18

Mom gets home a little early and is flapping around the house in crisis mode. "No one came by, did they?" she asks, midflap.

"No," I say. "Who would've?"

"No one," she says.

It's pretty obvious that there's something she's not telling me, so I have two choices: try to pry it out of her or maintain the committed ignorance-is-bliss mind-set that has gotten me so far in life. I don't pry, and she settles down after a while. There's not really anything she can do. She hasn't heard back from Mrs. DiMartino or the hospital, and I haven't heard back from Mars.

She's still wound up, though, and decides to take JR for a walk. It turns out he's exactly the same way with walks as he is with biscuits: He could've had one a minute before and you'd never know. Mom gets the leash and he gets up and starts twitching around in excitement, and it's like, Dude! We just went all the way to the frickin' pond and back, remember? You met Mr. and Mrs. Windbreaker and won the Nobel Beast Prize? But, nope, it's like he's never been out of the house before.

"You let him out today, right?" says Mom. "I mean, after the thing?"

The thing . . . Is that what she's going to call it?

"Yeah," I say. "I walked him halfway to Brantley!"

We both look at Johnny, and he gives us this wide-eyed who-me? look. And now Mom is thinking the same thing as me: dumb as a post with the memory of a goldfish, or a smooth operator who's got us right where he wants us? I feel like the evidence is shifting in his favor. Anyway, out they go, and I start to wonder when or if I'm going to get dinner.

I nuke some pizza rolls to hold me over, and it sort of feels weird to eat them all myself. I think about texting Mars again, but the ball is definitely in his court. The rules of the game are: If you hit it twice in a row, you lose. Mom comes home a half hour later and makes us macaroni and cheese.

I spend a long time online after that. I don't even know why I'm doing it until Janie's name pops up with the little green dot next to it — available to chat — and then it's like, Yep, that's why I'm here.

The room has gotten dark by now, so I sit there lit up by the computer screen and think about it. The ball is 100 percent in her court, too, but this game feels different. For one thing, it's been going on a lot longer. For another, I already feel like a loser. I remember the bike ride, the stupid hair gel, and her father, the prince of darkness, filling up the door frame.

Hey, I type.

Then I wait.

I wait my loser wait.

I sort of need her to reply. This day has kicked my butt and I need something good to happen. But I can't make it happen. I can't hit the same ball three times. That's pretty much unprecedented in human and tennis history.

I get up and turn on the light.

I sit back down.

I wait some more.

Hey, she types.

Now I'm like: What next? I'm trying to think of something funny or clever or at least not idiotic or pathetic, but she is typing again.

Heard you stopped by . . .
Didn't think he'd tell you!

She doesn't reply immediately, so I have time to reread my response about eight times. Was that pathetic? It was supposed to be a joke. Sort of. Maybe the exclamation point was too much?

She's typing: **I probably shouldn't tell you haw he phrased it!**

I read it twice. There's a typo and an exclamation point, and it's a joke. Sort of. It is the best response anyone has ever written in the history of online chats! And then I remember that I might be mad at her, and she is 100 percent on record as being mad at me.

Ha! I type, just to type something.

Then I type: **Were you home?**

I look at it. Delete it.

I'm back.

But she knows that already. Delete it.

How have you been?

Delete it.

I got a dog.

Send.

cool.

He's a rottweiler.

excellent

I'm waiting for her to ask me his name. She's not into punk rock or metal or anything like that. Just to be totally honest, she's one of those people who, if you said, "Music sucks right now," she would say, "What do you mean? What about sucky band X or sucky band Y?" But I still think she'll like the name. The other possibility is that she'll think it's mean. She's a lot nicer than I am.

He bit Mars :o

Delete it.

Her name pops up: **Gotta go!**

We must have been typing at the same time. And just like that, she's off-line. Unless her house is on fire or something, she chat-hung up on me. It sort of stings, but then I read back through and it doesn't seem so bad. She hit the ball back, maybe not directly into my court but at least in my general direction.

Anyway, it's amazing how easy it is to think of things to say now that she's off-line. I type out a long paragraph to her. I just kind of put it all out there. I think it's pretty good, all things considered. I read it over again. Delete it.

19

I barely sleep at all. I've been having trouble sleeping for a while now, but this one is bad even for me. By the time the phone rings at a little after seven on Friday morning, I've already been awake for hours. I think maybe I've been waiting for it.

Phone calls that come in very late or very early are pretty much always bad news. I get up and grab the closest, easiest things, the old sweatpants I was wearing last night and my battered NOFX T-shirt. Then I head for the stairs, moving in full spy mode. I sit down a few steps from the bottom. The phone in the hall is just around the corner from there, and my mom is already talking.

"Yes, Helen," she says.

Helen DiMartino.

"No, Helen."

I wonder if there's some reason she keeps saying her first name, like it's something she learned in one of her corporate seminars about Empowerment or Salesmanship or Dealing with Psychobilly Rednecks.

"I told you this yesterday . . . Yes . . . All of them. All of them and then some."

Mom listens for a while. Mrs. DiMartino is talking so loud that I can hear little bits of her voice all the way over here, but I can't make out what she's saying. She sounds like bees buzzing.

"No, absolutely not. Completely healthy. None of those things. He spent nearly a month at the vet's."

And now I know what they're talking about.

"Dr. Sanderson . . . Yes, Helen, I gave you the number. . . . No, absolutely not."

Her voice is getting more strained. Maybe it's what Mrs. DiMartino is saying or maybe it's just because she's been shouting in Mom's ear the whole time. Either way, the morning fog is starting to clear out of my head, and two things are pretty clear: 1) They want her to take JR to the vet to have him tested to see if he might've given Mars anything. Despite what Mom is saying – "completely healthy" and all that – I can't help thinking of all those old tick bites; 2) Mom doesn't want to take him there.

I don't want her to, either. It's not because of the tests, which would mean maybe drawing some blood. I can't imagine that would be a smooth process with JR, but I'm sure they have ways of getting it done. Maybe they'd drug him. A line pops into my head: "I wanna be sedated!" But that makes me think of what else they do at the vet's, the kind of sedation dogs don't wake up from.

By the time I tune back in to the phone call, Mom is saying, "Good-bye, Helen," and hanging up.

I hear her coming this way. I'm not sure if I should stand up or what, so I stay where I am. She jumps about three feet in the air when she sees me.

"Jesus, Jimmer!" she says. "You scared me."

"Sorry."

"Don't do that to me before I've had my coffee," she says, and then her tone shifts. "Did you hear?"

"Yeah," I say. "They should test Mars. See if he gave JR anything."

"I know," she says. "Go back to bed."

She heads off to the kitchen to get her coffee, and I head back upstairs. I try to go back to sleep for a while, but it's even more useless now than it was before the phone rang. I get up and get dressed. I get my best bad jeans and my black boots. I want to be ready in case I need to do something. I don't know what that would be, but that's why I want to be ready. I stick with the same T-shirt, though, because it's all-purpose.

As I'm putting on my second boot, I hear a car door slam, then a second one. I clomp over to the window, wearing one boot and holding the other, in time to see Mom backing out of the driveway. Oh crap. I rush downstairs, but the house is empty: no Mom, and no dog. It's just me, standing there in the living room with a boot in my hand.

Eventually, I make my way to the kitchen. There's a note on the refrigerator, but I already know what it's going to say. I pour myself some cereal, eat most of it, and sit there smashing the rest of it with my spoon. I've got the remains pulped and spread out over the surface like sugary pond scum when someone knocks on the door. If I were more alert, I'd be the one jumping three feet. As it is, I just look up. It's Rudy. He gives me a look through the glass like, You gonna open this?

Rudy is like a vampire: He'll only come in if he's invited. I think it's because his dad "values his privacy." Whenever I'm over there, we're always extra careful about knocking so we never have to find out what he's hiding. Whatever it is, I wave him in.

"You look like hell," he says.

"Thanks," I say. "Want the rest of my cereal?"

He looks into the bowl. "Nasty," he says. "Where's Killer?"

"Don't call him that."

"Sorry, just kidding."

"At the vet's."

"Damn . . . They're not . . ."

"I don't think so, just tests."

"Oh."

"To make sure Mars didn't give him anything."

Rudy laughs a little. "He's probably in the clear," he says. "Pretty sure Mars can't catch sexually transmitted diseases from himself."

Now I laugh, mostly out of relief. That joke is Rudy's way of saying, I'm on your side, not his.

"Thanks," I say.

"No problem," he says, but I'm not sure he really understands why I said it. "Anyway, I gotta hit the road. I'm picking up some extra money downtown. They need some muscle for the weekend deliveries at the market."

"They need some cheap labor, more like," I say.

"Can we agree on cheap muscle?"

"Small muscle, maybe."

"Don't be after any of my sweet, sweet spending money, then."

"All right, just try not to leave it out where I can see it," I say. "Hey . . ."

"Yeah?"

"What time you gonna be done?"

"I don't know," he says. "Afternoon."

"Stop by, all right? We'll hang with Killer."

If JR comes back — it just pops into my head, but I pop it right back out.

"Cool," says Rudy.

He leaves and I dump out my cereal and go back to waiting.

20

I hear three taps on the glass of the front door: *Tik. Tik. Tik.* It's kind of a spooky sound, nails on glass, and even though I basically know it's Rudy before I turn around, there's still something creepy about turning around to see who's tapping their fingernails on the glass behind you.

"Why didn't you just knock?" I say, opening the door.

"My knuckles are too powerful," he says. "I'd blow out the glass, probably kill a bunch of people."

"There's only one people here," I say. It's a little goofy, but I'm in a good mood. Mom came back around ten thirty this morning and JR came back with her, looking a bit spooked maybe, but not drugged up or, you know, dead. As soon as I saw them, I let out a breath I hadn't even realized I was holding in.

Mom had to head straight into work, already seriously late, so she couldn't really talk about the whats or whys of the trip. Since then JR and I have just been chilling out in the house. Before Rudy showed up, I was sitting here trying to think why I was so worried about this dog. I don't mean what I thought might happen at the vet's. You hear about that stuff all the time: Some big dog bites someone or goes after a poodle and has to be put to sleep. And in pretty much every movie or book I know of where there's a chance a dog will be put to sleep, that's exactly what happens. No, I mean, why do I care so much?

JR isn't even technically my dog. He's half my dog, and it wasn't that long ago that he felt like even less than that. But now that he's in trouble? Now that he gets taken away first thing in the morning and I don't even know if he's coming back? *Now* he feels like my dog. Because I know what that feels like. He's had it tough, and he didn't mean it anyway, and no one really has a clue about him. So, yeah. Sounds like my dog to me.

"Can I pet him?" says Rudy.

JR is standing a few feet away and seems calm enough, but it's still a good question. Rudy is wearing a long-sleeve T-shirt, which has a saying I probably shouldn't repeat and an arrow pointing down, so I say: "Put your sleeve over your hand. Just pull it down a little."

I sort of mime what I mean, and he does it.

"I feel like a lion tamer," he says.

He takes a step, reaches over, and pets JR. His hand is clenched up to hold the sleeve in place, so all he can do is push it around the top of JR's head. JR ducks down a little at first, but he doesn't move away, doesn't sever Rudy's hand at the wrist, and more or less acts like any other skittish, antisocial, punk rock dog would. After a few circular motions, Rudy removes his hand, JR lifts his head, and life goes on.

"Cool," he says. "I thought he didn't trust dudes?"

"I think he can tell we're not, like, adults."

"That's kind of insulting," says Rudy. "But I guess it's true. At least for you."

"Yeah, he should be a bartender. He'd just eat the fake IDs."

"He's a lot friendlier than last time anyway."

"Depends," I say.

"Yeah, seriously," he says. "You heard anything from Mars?"

"No, and I texted him yesterday. It seriously was not that bad!"

"Yeah, he's a drama queen."

"I just hope he doesn't cause too much trouble. I have to deal with it, either way. Maybe I'll try him again later. It's a new day, I guess."

"Let me try him," says Rudy, and I immediately realize that's the way to go.

"Yeah, yeah!" I say. "Just ask him if he's OK. And maybe ask it in a way that he'd be a total wuss if he said no."

"Think I should call, then, or text?"

"Either way," I say. A text is good because I could show people the reply, but a call is OK too, because Rudy is, like, a semi-impartial witness.

"Right now?"

"No, wait, let me think about this for a minute," I say.

It feels like maybe there's some sort of strategy or trick I could use. I try to think about it but nothing is coming to me. What would they do to Mars in a movie? Shoot him. That doesn't help.

"Well, while you're waiting," he says.

He steps back toward the door.

"Don't open it all the way," I say, because JR is still in the room.

He opens the door just enough to wedge his body through. JR watches it open, but he doesn't make a break for it. And just like that, Rudy's back. Even before he pulls his left arm back inside, I can tell there's something in it. It's a little fishing pole, like the cheap plastic kind that every kid around here had at one time or other. I had one, but it broke. Because it was cheap and plastic.

"I found it in the stockroom!" he says.

"Do they sell those at the market?" I say.

"Well, they did at some point."

"And you went to work wearing that shirt?"

"Yeah, why not? I was just working in the back."

"Yeah, that one's actually kind of appropriate for 'working in the back,'" I say. "Does that thing have a hook and stuff?"

"Yeah, it's fully functional," he says. "You still have yours?"

"My hook?" I say, trying to trick him into saying "your pole."

He's too smart, though, or at least too experienced with sexual innuendo.

"You know what I mean," he says.

"Yeah," I say, "but I don't have any of that stuff anymore."

"Well," he says, looking down at the pole. "We got one hook. . . ."

"Wouldn't be any trouble to find a few night crawlers after all the rain yesterday. . . ."

"You want to?"

"Yeah, sure," I say. "What d'you think, just down to the pond?"

"Yeah, why not?"

"Because we're not eight anymore, and there's no way we'll catch anything worthwhile with that thing," I say. "It's a frickin' toy."

"Nice day, though," he says.

He's right about that.

"OK, let's go."

"Think we should take Killer here?"

JR is still looking at the edge of the door, where it used to be open.

"Sure," I say. "I've already taken him that far a few times. But we should probably stop calling him that, you know, all things considered."

Rudy looks at me.

"Public relations — image matters," I say. I saw that on a folder Mom brought home once. It's the sort of phrase that is obviously true but also makes you never want to work in an office in your life.

"Public Image Limited," says Rudy.

"Much better," I say.

PiL is Johnny Rotten's band after the Sex Pistols.

"Anger is an energy," says Rudy. It's a line from "Rise," one of their best songs.

"You could be right," I say, another line from it.

The good thing about getting into these bands way late is that you really only have to listen to their best stuff. I listen to some new bands, too, but they keep letting me down and going mainstream. Anyway, it's kind of a cool exchange.

And then we head out to go fishing with one hook, a kid's toy, a dog on a bright blue leash, and the beginnings of something like a plan.

"We can call Mars from there."

21

"Well, ain't we a couple o' rednecks?" says Rudy as we walk along the bike path behind town, heading toward the pond. JR isn't paying much attention to either of us. His world is at the end of his leash, and his senses are working overtime as he sorts through the sights and sounds and smells.

"Yeah, right?" I say. "We goin' down the crick, do us some fishin'!"

We make fun of it, but we keep walking straight there. We're quiet for a while, and I try to concentrate on what I'm doing. I stay even with JR and don't let him tug on his leash too much, and I stand up straight and don't make any sudden movements.

"You look like you have a stick up your butt," says Rudy.

"I'm working on my 'calm, assertive energy,'" I tell him.

"Your what?"

"I've been watching a lot of *Dog Whisperer* reruns," I say.

"Oh right," he says. "The timeless wisdom of basic cable. What's that guy's name again?"

"Cesar Millan," I say.

"Right. You still look like you've got a stick up your butt."

"Maybe I do."

Ten minutes later, we're at the pond. It's small, shallow, and choked with vegetation. "Well," I say. "We have an excellent chance of catching some really primo weeds in there."

"Yeah," says Rudy, looking down at the little fishing pole in his hand. "There's about a one hundred percent chance we're going to lose this hook."

"Well," I say, "let's at least kill a worm first."

Before I can start turning over rocks and pawing around for night crawlers, I have to figure out what to do with JR. As soon as we stopped, he turned around, figuring we were heading back from here, like we'd done before. It was one of those weird moments of dog intelligence that sort of catches you off guard. Or it caught me off guard anyway. We aren't heading back, though, so now he's just watching us talk and looking down the slope at the pond.

I look down the slope, too. There's a stubby, half-drowned tree jutting out of the bank and leaning over the water. "Why don't we go down there, and I'll tie the leash up to the tree?"

"What," says Rudy, "you think he'd run away?"

"Well, not from us, I don't think," I say. "I mean, not like a jailbreak, but if he sees a chipmunk or something, we'll never see him again."

"Or it," says Rudy.

"Yeah, right?"

We head down the slope. JR is like, All right, let's go there. He takes the lead, pulling on the leash in a way that I'm pretty sure is going to result in me rolling most of the way down. I lean way back instead, and when he stops at the bottom, I fall on my butt.

"Smooth," says Rudy, as JR begins slurping up pond water.

I wait for him to stop and then loop his leash around the trunk of the little tree. He watches me do it, realizes he isn't going anywhere, and lies down. Meanwhile, I go about the not especially difficult work of finding a good, fat worm.

"Man," I say, slowly working a five-incher out of the dirt. "This place is crawling with 'em."

"That's what you like to hear," says Rudy. "Pond-side views, crawling with worms, must see!"

"You're going to end up just like them," I say, meaning his parents.

He strikes a superhero pose and points his finger at the sky. "Never!"

"You've got the real-estate gene on both sides."

"They can fix that now," he says. "Nanosurgery."

"Nope, you're inoperable. Might as well add your name to the sign: M&S&R Realty."

"Don't even say that, man. That is just . . . I will drown myself right here in this pond."

"I'll help."

He laughs. "Nice," he says. "Let's catch some fish."

"All right," I say. "Give me the pole."

"Does that line work for you?"

"Yeah, ha-ha. Seriously, I've got a thick five-incher here that needs it bad."

"That's sad," he says. "I'm holding a three-foot rod that — Oh, wait, should we call Mars first?"

"Oh yeah," I say. My good mood goes out like a light, and I toss the worm into the grass halfway up the bank, a last-second pardon. "Yeah, let's."

Rudy takes out his phone. "Why are we doing this, exactly?"

"Dude, they're going to make my mom pay for the hospital and who knows what else," I say. I don't tell him the other thing I'm worried about. It sort of seems like saying it would make it more real, and I'd like to keep that thought firmly in the realm of paranoid delusion.

"I thought you said it wasn't that bad?"

"It isn't, but you know him — his whole family."

"Oh right," he says. "Definitely don't want to give them a blank check."

"At all. Mom is pretty stressed about that stuff already."

"What stuff?"

"Money stuff. Her office is The Suck right now."

"Oh," he says. "Got it."

"I just want to get him on record as still having all his fingers and not suffering 'emotional distress' or whatever they're going to try to bill us for."

"He's not going to say anything like that," says Rudy. "Since when has Mars ever talked about his emotions?"

"Yeah, I know," I say. "But if he just says he's OK or it's no big deal or something like that, that's a good start."

"Yeah," says Rudy. "I could see him doing that. . . . You just want, like, confirmation of his OK-ness. So, call or text?"

"Let's call. You're, like, my witness. Maybe you can get him talking."

"OK," he says. "I'll put it on speaker."

"Cool," I say. I turn to JR and make the shush sign, which there's a decent chance he'll understand. The last thing we need is him barking at Mars's voice and giving us away, but he's conked out already. He's lying on his side and soaking up the sunlight in his black fur like a big, drooling solar cell.

Rudy hits speaker. The air is warm and still and I can hear the ringing pretty clearly. Once, twice, three times, and just when I'm expecting it to go to voice mail, Mars picks up.

"Hey, jerk-off," he says to Rudy, who pulls the phone closer to his head to talk.

Rudy's response is less polite, and once the formalities are out of the way, he gets right down to business. "How's the mitt, man?"

There's a long pause. Just say it's fine and get this over with, I think.

"I don't know," Mars says. His voice sounds small and far away over the speaker. I kick the dirt and Rudy looks over at me. JR raises his head.

"God, just grow a pair," says Rudy. For a second, I think he's talking to me.

"Easy for you to say," says Mars. "Dog practically ripped my hand off."

I form the words "that's bull" slowly, so that Rudy can see them.

"Exaggerate much?" he says into the phone.

"Whatever," says Mars. "My mom says it'll probably get infected."

"Yeah, right," I mouth.

"Your mom?" says Rudy. "What about the doctor?"

Rudy has a point. Mars's mom is basically the opposite of a doctor: uneducated and harmful. Mars doesn't answer, so Rudy tries again. "I hear it wasn't really that bad."

It wasn't, I'm thinking. And he hopped the fence and provoked it.

"Yeah," says Mars. "Where'd you hear that, Jimmer?"

"Could be," says Rudy.

"Yeah, well, who's gonna believe him?" says Mars.

And there it is. Rudy looks over at me and grimaces: He's got you there.

Mars is still going: "Maybe we should ask his 'aunt'. . . ."

"Yeah, yeah," says Rudy.

"Hey, where are you right now?" says Mars.

"On the couch," says Rudy, looking out at the pond.

"Why don't I come over and play some Kinect?" says Mars.

"You up to it?" says Rudy. There's a splash farther down the shore, some turtle or duck or something. Rudy covers the phone with his other hand, but it's too late. I don't know if Mars heard, but he's quiet for a few seconds.

"I can beat you with one hand," he says, finally. But he sounds different now, more cautious. Stupid turtle.

"Nah, Xbox's broken," Rudy says. "Anyway, I got some stuff to do. Just wanted to check in."

"Yeah," says Mars. "All right. Check ya later."

"All right," Rudy says. He hangs up.

"Dammit," I say.

"Yeah," says Rudy. "He's pretty smart, for an idiot."

"That's such bull," I say. "All of it."

I kick the ground again, harder this time. The first worm has made its escape, so I find another one.

"You know," says Rudy as he impales the night crawler on the hook, folds it back, and skewers it again. "If there's anything you want to tell me about this summer, this might be a good time."

I make a screw-you-very-much face, but I'm actually thinking about it. And then, just like that, he casts the line out into the pond. The red-and-white plastic bobber lands with a little splash. JR gets up to investigate as Rudy and I sit down to start watching it. After about fifteen minutes without even a nibble, he hands me the pole and it's my turn to "fish."

22

I've got a bite!

As soon as I start reeling it in, I can feel it's not much. Probably just a dumb sunfish, the annoying bait stealers that have always been the enemy of any worthwhile fishing around here. Still, it's been years since I've reeled anything in and it's sort of fun.

"Lucky!" says Rudy.

He just handed me the pole a few minutes ago, and the timing and the fact that he is so obviously jealous make this even more fun. The little fish comes into view as I pull it closer to the surface, but it's hard to see it clearly because of the ripples the line is causing. Finally, I tug it out of the pond, and we can see it flapping around on the end of the line.

"Sunfish," says Rudy. "Nothing."

JR disagrees. He's been moving around over by his tree, and now that the little fish is out of the water, I risk a look back. He's at the end of his leash, staring at the fish. His mouth is hanging open and as he snaps it shut to start barking, a thick lasso of drool slips off and flies through the air. Rudy sees it, too.

"I think he's hungry," he says.

"He's always hungry," I say.

JR barks at the fish a few more times as I raise the pole and swing it toward me, but once I grip the thing in my hand and start trying to work the hook out, JR's mouth shuts and his eyes get wider than I've ever seen them.

"Hey, dude," says Rudy. "Eyes on the prize."

We only have one hook, so I concentrate on working it free. It's not in deep. The little fish is slick in my hand but it's not as cold as I expected. It must've been in the warm water near the surface. It fits easily in my hand, so keeping it still isn't a problem like it was when I was seven and trying to wrestle with a trout. The hook pops out.

As I swing my hand back to toss the thing into the pond, I hear JR's leash tearing the bark off the tree. I turn around just to make sure he hasn't pulled the whole thing up by its roots. He looks at me, looks at the fish, looks at me.

"Do it," says Rudy. "Seriously."

Now, the thing to do with sunfish is throw them back. They're too small to keep and too bony anyway. But I guess that's human thinking.

"Really?" I say.

"Yeah," says Rudy. "Why not?"

I look around like there might be a game warden watching us from behind a tree.

"I don't know," I say. I feel the fish in my hand, still trying to flap and slap its way to freedom. "Kind of cruel."

"To what, the fish?" says Rudy. "Is there any species that's ever been treated worse? And anyway, look at your dog. It's kind of cruel to show him this fish and then just throw it back."

I picture JR, his look of confusion as the fish splashes back into the pond and disappears, confusion and then profound dog sorrow. What the heck. I turn and deliver the fish with a short, underhand toss. He gathers his back legs underneath him, like he does for a biscuit, but he's still leashed to the tree.

"Nononono!" I say, but it's too late.

He launches himself into the air. His jaws snap down on the fish in midair, a split second before he reaches the end of his leash.

The fish is like: Freedom! Dog! *Arrrr!*

JR is like: Fish! Leash! *Yoink!*

He's yanked backward — I hear the tree creak from his weight — and he crashes back to the ground. But his jaws never stop working. He's literally chewing as he falls. By the time he stands back up again, he's licking his lips. His thick pink tongue swipes out and over, looking for any last traces of fish.

"Whoa!" I say.

"He obliterated that thing," says Rudy, and his tone is just pure awe.

"Well," I say, reviewing my decision. "I don't think it suffered."

"That was the coolest thing," says Rudy. "Maybe ever."

I can't think of anything to add, so I don't.

"All right," says Rudy after a while. "My turn."

"Fine," I say. "You go find a worm."

"No problem. This place is crawling with them."

A few minutes later, JR is lying down in the sun again for some solar-powered digestion, and Rudy is settling in for what I expect to be a long turn with the fishing pole. I'm just watching the water, checking my phone, watching the water, scratching my neck, watching the water, swatting a mosquito, scratching the bite, checking my phone.

"I think I got —" says Rudy.

I sit up.

"Nothing."

I slouch back down. The sun feels good on my face. It looks like I'll get some color this summer after all.

"Not a bad Friday," says Rudy.

"Not at all, especially considering it's our last one." School starts Monday.

"Dude, don't even talk about that. Seriously. I'm not ready."

"You and me both," I say.

Just the thought of those hallways, those people, the crowds in between classes, and the smell of whatever it is they use to semi-clean the place . . . It makes my stomach want to implode.

"OK, let's settle this," says Rudy. "Neither of us talks about Monday until Monday."

"Deal," I say. "Except I'm going to need a ride."

"OK, starting now," he says. "Yeah, I figured you would. OK. Now."

I make a lip-zipping motion with my right hand. It feels a little stiff with fish slime, so I wipe it on my jeans again. A few minutes later, we hear people up on the path, heading our way. We both sort of straighten up, and JR gets to his feet. If it's anyone we know, Rudy will probably start acting like this is all a big joke, waving the pole around like he's trying to break it. And I'll probably act like I just stumbled across this impossibly lame scene. But it's not anyone we know, not really, anyway.

"Is that Johnny down there?" calls Mr. F.

Mrs. F. peers down at us, probably scanning the pond's edge for firearms, meth pipes, or prostitutes.

"Yep," I say.

It's no longer Windbreaker weather, and I'm sort of relieved that their shirts don't match, too.

Rudy takes one hand off the pole and gives them half a wave.

"Catch anything?" says Mr. F.

"Caught a sunfish, but that guy ate it," I say, nodding toward JR.

"Which guy?" says Mr. F.

"Oh, Hank," says his wife, her weapons inspection complete.

JR fires off a warning bark at Mr. F., but they just think he's saying hi. Then he goes back to lying down, like he can't be bothered with this.

"Well, we'll leave you to it," says Mrs. F.

"Hope you catch something," says Mr. F.

"Hope you catch syphilis," says Rudy, under his breath.

"What's that?" says Mrs. F.

"Nothing," Rudy says. "Thanks!"

They wave good-bye to us and then to JR, who raises his head and looks up the slope at them. Happy with that, they wander off down the path, and we go back to not catching anything. JR goes back to lying in the sun. A few minutes later, his eyes are closed and his side is moving up and down as he breathes.

School is off the list of approved subjects, talking about Mars would just make me angry, and there's nothing doing out here.

It doesn't seem like there's anything left to say. Turns out, I'm wrong.

"So," Rudy says in that wading-into-something way.

"Yeah?"

"Saw Janie downtown."

"When, today?"

"Yeah."

"Didn't you just see her the other day?"

"I don't think that was me, dude."

"Oh yeah," I say. It was Aaron.

"Anyway," says Rudy. "It's not like I'm stalking her."

No, I am. JR's legs kick a few times and he makes a weird little noise, but his eyes stay closed the whole time. He's dreaming. It's either about chasing something, or being chased.

"What was she doing?" I ask, looking back at Rudy.

"Jumping jacks," he says. "What d'you think? She was working."

"She works downtown?"

"Wait, you didn't know that?"

"No, where?"

"Yeah," says Rudy. "She works at that garden place. Has all summer. Anyway, it's right across from the market. She was working out front, and I saw her on my way in."

"How'd she look?" I say.

"Dirty," he says.

"Shut up, man."

"No, literally. She was taking plants out of little plastic things and putting them in pots. She was dirty, like dirt dirty."

"Oh," I say. "That's cool."

"It's not."

"And she's been there all summer?" I say. I sort of wonder how much money she's been making and what she's been doing with it. Dracula probably has her putting half of it away for college.

"Yeah, I think," says Rudy. "Again, not stalking."

We go back to fishing for a while, even though all it really amounts to is watching the little plastic bobber float on the surface. I sort of forgot about this part. When I think of fishing when I was a kid, I think of catching a few things and opening day at the lake and that little snack bar they have. Fishing is, like, 98 percent waiting, but I only remember the other 2 percent.

"You should stop by," says Rudy.

"You think?"

"Yeah, just buy a plant or something."

"What do I need a plant for?"

"You don't, moron, but just buy one and say hi."

"Oh yeah. How much is a plant? Like a small one?"

"The hell would I know?"

"I don't know," I say. "You work right across the parking lot."

"Yeah, like a day or two a week. Anyway, it's a garden store, so they have other things besides plants."

"Like what?" I say.

"Like rakes," he says, and then he breaks into a smile. "And hoes."

"Watch it, dude," I say, but that was pretty good.

"Anyway, you should go soon," he says. "This is probably her last weekend."

We're so perilously close to talking about school starting up again that I figure I might as well.

"I don't know," I say. "I'll see her in school."

Rudy starts to say something, stops, then says it anyway: "You sure about that?"

I'm not. It's not a big school, but it's big enough for one person to ignore another.

We go back to fishing. A few false alarms later, we lose our hook in the weeds.

"Stupid weeds!" I shout. "You'll pay for that."

"Yeah, that'll be three cents, please," says Rudy.

JR opens his eyes to see what the noise is about, and then he stands up. It's like he knows it's time to go, too. It's probably past time. My face feels hot and tight from all the sun.

"Dude, is my face —?"

"Like a lobster," says Rudy.

He already had some color, so his looks pretty much the same. I untie JR's leash from the tree. He shakes his head to clear the dog dreams out and we all head up the slope. Halfway home, Rudy peels off and heads for his place.

"Later," I say.

"Yep," he says. He takes the pole with him.

Then it's just JR and me.

"You have a good rest, boy?" It doesn't seem weird to talk to him when I'm alone. I don't know if he's really listening, but I'm pretty sure he's not judging me for it. "I don't know what you're resting from. Other resting, I guess."

He stops and marks a bush with processed pond water.

"Liked that fish, didn't ya?"

I don't say anything else the rest of the way, and neither does he. When we reach the backyard, I look at the fence, at the spot where Mars must've hopped it. Then I flip the latch on the gate and we head inside. I know JR probably wants to hit the water dish and then head to his spot in the living room, so I reach down to undo his leash.

He turns back to look at exactly the same time, and suddenly my face is right next to his. By the time I realize what I've done, it's already too late.

23

His mouth comes up fast, way too fast for me to get out of the way. There's nothing I can do. His mouth snaps open, and *he licks me.*

He gets the side of my chin, the corner of my mouth, and some of my nose.

"Aw!" I sputter. "Man!"

Dog slobber — with a whiff of sunfish! I wipe the back of my hand across the bottom of my face. It's the first time he's done that, the first time he's licked my face, just like a normal dog. It's kind of disgusting, but I don't mind at all.

24

I walk downtown on Saturday morning. Maybe I'm going to see Janie, maybe I'm not. I don't even know if she's working today. Either way, it's the second-to-last day of summer vacation, and I feel like doing something. I didn't have a job this summer, obviously, but I didn't spend much, either. Add it all up, and I've got a twenty-dollar bill in my wallet and I sort of feel like spending it.

Halfway there, I get a text from Rudy. He called Aaron, looking for secondhand info on Mars, but he didn't get any: **Nothing from A. Boxed out.** Aaron has always been good at keeping his mouth shut. I reply: **Thnx man. Heading downtown.**

In da car, he writes. Since it's Saturday morning, he's probably going food shopping with his folks at the big Price Chopper out by the interstate.

OK, later, I text.

It's extremely cool of Rudy to do all this slick spy work for me. I know he hung out with those two a lot this summer, but it sort of feels like the battle lines have been drawn now, and I really appreciate him coming back to my side. Not like I thought he'd choose them, but he definitely could've stayed neutral.

I reach the edge of downtown, cross over on to the sidewalk, and pass the first few stores. It's another nice day, and the sun is hitting the big, clean front windows of the shops. People are walking along the sidewalks and walkways, staying inside the lines. Cars are rolling slowly through town, stopping at the cross-walk, moving on. No one seems to be in a hurry, and everything seems so small-town perfect you could just puke, you know? I make the difficult decision not to vomit and just go with it.

I've got two more days of vacation and a twenty to spend, and I'm hoping this whole thing with JR will be over soon. Mom didn't have much to say when she got back from work last night, only that she took JR to the vet to get retested and that she was sure everything was fine, "like it was the last time I took him."

He'd already gotten his shots and vaccinations and all that stuff, so no rabies or anything crazy like that. And the bite itself wasn't much, so what's left, right? I still haven't heard from Mars, and Mom never heard back from his parents after the trip to the vet, because what could they really say? We'll just wait till the hos-pital sends out the bill on Monday or whenever and pay for some fresh bandages and whatever junk they bought in the gift shop.

Give it a week and things will be back to normal. The battle lines will disappear, and I probably won't have to worry about Mars dropping by and eating all my snacks for a while. It's a win-win. Unless it's not, but right now that's the way I'm trying to look at it.

I head into the little coffee place to get a small one to go and maybe a snack. Mom and Rudy both say coffee's an "acquired taste," and I'm trying to acquire it. It seems like a cooler way to get my caffeine than Mountain Dew. I'm sixteen now; I can't drink bright green soda forever.

It's midmorning and the tables are all full, but the line isn't too bad. I get the coffee to go and load it up with milk and sugar. I get a large chocolate chip cookie, in case the coffee is still too bitter, but it isn't. I sit outside on the coffee shop's one bench, eat the cookie, and drink half the coffee. It's not so bad with all the sugar in it. Then I get up and start walking toward the garden store.

I have an idea of how I want this to go: I'll be walking by, casually sipping my coffee like some dude from France, and will just happen to look in the window. What do you know? There's Janie. We'll make eye contact and I'll head in. Just to say hi, no big deal. I'll push open the door and maybe there's an old lady with her arms full of flowers, so I'll hold it open for her and everyone will see me do it. Once she's gone, I'll make some funny comment and everyone will laugh, especially Janie.

That's the general plan anyway, but I'm walking so slow that I run out of coffee before I get there. I consider going back for another one, but I figure I can still hold the cup, and this way, there's zero chance of spilling when I open the door.

I cross the parking lot and spot the door – worn green paint and a dull metal handle. I begin my approach, moving even slower now. It's just that I haven't seen Janie in a really long time and, I think I mentioned this, it did not go well the last time I did. Plus, I still haven't figured out what I'm going to do in there. I mean, apart from dazzling everyone with a funny line that I haven't thought of yet.

I guess I'll buy a plant, like Rudy said, but what if she's not there? Would I still have to buy one? I guess I could be like: Give me your smallest, most hard-core, lowest-maintenance plant, please. Or maybe I could buy some gardening gloves or plant food or whatever's cheapest. And just like that, I'm past the door now.

The walkway in front is gravel, so I sound like a bowl of Rice Krispies as I walk past the window. I look in and there she is. She's standing behind the counter and looking out, bored. Just like that, she sees me. I see her see me: Her head turns and stops. I don't even realize I've stopped moving until I register the lack of snap, crackle, and pop from the gravel. We make eye contact through the glass. Wasn't that part of my plan?

It was, but not like this. I'm heading the wrong way. If I turn around now, it will be the opposite of casual, the opposite of cool. And where's my coffee cup? I close my fingers to make sure it's still there and feel the paper sides crumple in my hand.

I don't know what to do, but I have to do something. I go forward just because that's the direction I'm headed, but once I start, I feel like that's that. I can't boomerang back. Which doesn't explain why I was in front of the store in the first place. I reach the end of the walkway and there's nothing left to do but head back across the parking lot.

Maybe she watches me go and maybe she doesn't. Her image is still in my mind: her head turning and then stopping as she sees me, her eyes a mystery at that distance. I have no idea what she was thinking. Was she happy to see me? Angry? Annoyed? I don't know. She looked good, though. She had a nice tan and her hair was a little lighter. That's probably from the sun, too.

I'm thinking about all this as I'm passing by CVS. Out of the corner of my eye, I see someone shoulder through the door and stop dead. I turn to look: It's Mars. His arm is in a brand-new sling, the material so white, it seems to glow in the sunlight. That snake.

25

"I don't want to talk to you," says Mars.

I haven't even said anything to him yet. It's a preemptive strike, but he's not getting off that easy.

"Yeah, if you open your mouth too wide, some of the bull —" I start, but I stop and start over. I remember the situation and, even though it's a total kick in the crotch, I force myself to dial it back. "What's that thing for?"

He looks down at the sling. From his expression, you'd think he'd never seen it before, but I know that's not why he looks so confused. He's trying to figure out how to explain it to me, the one person who knows how ridiculous it is. It's, like, a special hand sling. The slings I've seen before, like on football players at school, let the hand hang out the front. They're just made to keep the arm or the elbow still, I guess. But the end of this one is closed off, so that the hand is stuffed in there. I can see his knuckles pushing out against the white fabric near the end.

"You know what it's for," he says.

"No, I really don't," I say. "It was just a little bite. Dude, I *saw* it."

Someone comes through the door, and we have to move aside, a little off the walkway.

"You didn't get a good look," he says. He hasn't looked me in the eyes yet.

"I cleaned it up and put a bandage on it!"

"Two," Mars says.

"Yeah, two little bandages," I say. "I'm sorry I was all out of Winnie-the-Pooh ones. Where'd you get that thing?"

"The hospital," he says.

"From the doctor?"

He doesn't answer.

"You got it in the frickin' gift shop, didn't you?" I say. The gift shop in the hospital sells stuff for recovering patients. I had a reaction to a yellow-jacket sting when I was a kid, and Mom bought me a "pirate" eye patch there. I was too young to realize it was just a regular eye patch. I don't even need to wait for Mars to answer to know I'm right. "Can't wait to see that on the bill."

"Shut up, man," he says, and now he does look me in the eyes.

I crossed a line there, reminding him that his mom was going to be sending a bill to mine. He's touchy about his family, even though he's just like them.

"Take that thing off," I say.

"Why?" he says.

"Because you don't need it," I say.

"Maybe I do."

"You don't, and you know it."

"You don't know what I know," he says. "You just don't want everyone to find out what a psycho that stupid dog of yours is. He's a hazard, man. He's dangerous."

"Only if you make him," I say.

"What?" he says. "Shut up."

"You hopped the fence," I say. "I know you did. You cornered him. He's a rescue, man. You can't do that. That's all on you."

"What? No way," he says, but then he can't help himself. "Wait, did you see?"

I start to respond, but he must realize what he just said, and he cuts me off.

"Because there wasn't anything to see!" he says. "I was outside it, and he jumped up!"

"Yeah, is that the official story?" I say. I'm about to cross the same line again, but I can't help it. I'm so mad at him right now. I have seventeen bucks and change left, and I'd give all of it to punch him right in the head. I wonder how he'd put a sling on that. "Is that what your mom is telling you to say?"

I can see that one land. It's solid contact, a direct hit, but he shakes it off.

"Yeah, you'd know all about that kind of thing, huh?" he says. "Official stories?"

"Shut up, man," I say. "Seriously."

"Seriously," he says, imitating my voice, but making it higher.

I see his eyes dart to the side, so mine do the same. People are stopping and watching. One guy has shopping bags in both arms and a couple has matching strollers in front of them. A few others are just standing there. They think there might be a fight. I don't know if they're getting ready to step in or if they just want a free show. And I'd love to give them one, but I can't. For one thing, he's wearing a sling, and even if it's total bull, they don't know that. They probably think I'm the reason he's wearing it in the first place. And two, I've got to dial it back again, because he's got something over me right now. He can cause real problems. I exhale.

"Sorry, man," I say.

It catches him off guard. It sort of catches me off guard, too. I wasn't sure I was going to be able to do it.

"What?" he says.

It takes all my willpower, but I double down. "Sorry, I just got a little — you know how I get — how's it feeling? The hand?"

He looks down at it, stuffed like a sausage into the end of the sling. The people start to move away. By the time he looks up again, he's figured me out. He's got that look in his eyes, that trickster look, the one he has when he's about to do something crazy.

"I'm not an idiot, you know," he says.

He shoulders past me, with his "good" shoulder. He doesn't bump me hard, but it's not soft, either.

"And just so you know," he says as he goes, "you're going to be getting more than a bill for this. A lot more."

I head straight home after that. I even run part of the way, but I give that up pretty quick. This isn't the sort of thing I can out-run, and by the time I find my mom out in the yard, she already knows. I start to tell her about the sling and what he said and how he said it, but she shakes her head.

"I know," she says.

"Well, I don't! What does it mean?"

She looks down. It feels like a lot of people have been avoiding looking me in the eyes today. She's speaking low and looking at the grass, but I don't have any trouble hearing her.

"I found out right after you left," she says. "They're suing. We're going to court."

26

"Court," I say. "Like *Judge Judy*?"

That question probably doesn't capture just how mad I am right now, but it does a pretty good job of capturing, you know, what the heck do I know about getting sued? All I know are the crazy stories that make it into the news, like the one about the guy who fell through a skylight trying to break into a house and then sued the guy he was trying to rob.

And it always seems like people are suing for these huge, fantasy-land amounts of money, millions of dollars, because their herbal tea was too hot or the dry cleaner lost their pants. I should probably get less of my news online, but the more I think about it, the madder I get.

I'm trying to ask Mom more questions, but I'm too mad to talk. And then I remember Mars and that smug look on his face: "You're going to be getting more than a bill. . . ." He already knew, Mom had already heard, and I was still clueless, still trying to be *nice* to him. Now I really want to punch someone, but Mom is the only one out here, and she's one of the few people I don't want to hit.

I spot an old bobblehead figure that Mom rescued from the trash and put out by the little cement birdbath like an extra sporty garden gnome. I got the thing at a baseball game when I was a kid.

Back then I could have been anything: a baseball player, a bobblehead collector, anything. But the last sport to interest me at all was skateboarding, and that was years ago, and the only thing I collect now is loud music. So I threw the bobblehead out as part of a larger room purge last year. And Mom rescued it, and now I have it again. For a second, I'm just holding it in my hand. The head bounces stupidly on its rusty spring, the blue cap going up and down, like: Yes, do it.

"Oh, don't," says Mom, but she says it softly, and that just makes me madder.

My hand goes up and then comes down hard as I throw the thing at the concrete base of the birdbath. It's a direct hit. The fat little body goes one way, the head goes another, and the spring splits the difference. I turn back toward Mom. I don't know if I feel better, but at least I can get the words out now.

"They're suing?" I say.

She looks at me for a moment, then looks around at the broken pieces. Finally, she just shakes her head.

"They're looking for money," she says. "I can't say I'm surprised."

"Like, millions?" I say.

"Not millions," she says. Stupid Internet.

"So what, then?" I say. "I mean . . . what?"

"We're going to have to go to court," she says. She sizes up the blank look on my face, takes a breath, and continues. "They'll ask for what they think they can get, probably more, and your uncle Greg will help us."

Greg is Mom's brother. He has defended murderers, even a mobster once.

"Wait, do we go to court against, like, the state?" I ask. "Or against them?"

"Against them," she says.

"But what can they even — Mars jumped the fence!"

"That's not what they say."

And I can't prove it. My head is swimming. How do a few bandages turn into a sling? How does a bite on the hand turn into a lawsuit? None of it makes any sense, but I guess it's the law, so it doesn't have to. There just has to be money involved.

I look up at Mom. She looks sad and tired. She's standing in the middle of the lawn and the house is directly behind her. She's centered in it, like it's a picture frame floating in the air. That's the thing, I realize, the house — the mortgage that's been hanging over her head. I don't know all the details, but it's called an adjustable rate mortgage, and a few years ago, the rates adjusted a ton. We could lose the house over this.

"Dammit!" I shout, and then I shout something worse.

Mom flinches the first time, at the volume, but not the second. Inside the house, JR starts barking. He heard me. Maybe he even thinks I'm in trouble. He has no way of knowing how backwards he's got it.

27

Someone knocks on the door on Sunday morning, and JR starts barking again. It's not that early, but between getting sued, the failed walk-by with Janie, school starting up on Monday, and the Inherent Unfairness of the Universe I slept for crap, and I wouldn't have minded the opportunity to at least try to sleep in.

You know it's bad when you're hoping it's Jehovah's Witnesses, but when I look out the window, there's an oversized cream-white BMW in our driveway. It's Greg's car — Greg's latest car. To me it looks like the automotive equivalent of a pimp suit, but I'm sure he'd argue that it just "presents the right image." Greg argues everything. He's my uncle, Mom's brother, and our lawyer. I'm not surprised he's here, but I still get a really bad feeling as I look down at his pimpmobile.

I hear a fresh explosion of barking downstairs. It's JR, of course, but I've never heard him like this before. Even a floor away, the barks sound raw and angry. I throw on the same clothes from yesterday, with a clean pair of socks, and head down the stairs. By the time I reach the first floor, the barking has stopped, and I can hear Mom and Greg talking in the kitchen.

I walk through the doorway, and there's Greg, overdressed as usual. JR is nowhere in sight.

"Jimmer," Greg says, nodding.

"Hey, man," I say, and nod back.

I'm not sure about this — it's not the kind of thing that's big in what's left of our family — but I think he might be my godfather. That would be appropriate, considering what I know about his mobbed-up clients. And apart from the family stuff, I've already seen a lot of him this year; he was my lawyer, too.

He turns back toward Mom to continue talking. Mom looks businesslike. You can see that she's been up for a while. She's already washed, already dressed for the day, already fully caffeinated. Greg is her older brother, but I guess it's still a meeting with her lawyer. Mom is not the kind of person to ever fail for lack of effort.

"I need some time with the animal," Greg says, and that snaps me back. The "animal"? Like he's a wombat or something.

"His name's JR," I say. "And where is he?"

"Out back," says Mom. "He's not a big fan of his legal representation."

Greg lets out a small laugh, and we all head toward the back door and straight through. Mom's in front, I'm next, and Greg is last in line.

"Careful where you step," Mom calls back to Greg.

JR is in a spot near the back corner. He's sitting down when I see him, but as soon as Greg appears behind me, he stands up and starts barking. He looks angrier than I've ever seen him. He's pointing his mouth up and really going for it. His jaws snap shut in between loud, rasping barks, and his eyes are wide open and staring at Greg, who has the good sense to stay halfway in the door.

Mom makes a beeline for JR. For a second, I think maybe I should hold her back, but he barely notices her. Even as she reaches him, his eyes stay on Greg.

"He doesn't trust grown men," she shouts over her shoulder. "Bad history."

She grabs JR's collar and gives it a hard tug. "Hey!" she says.

I'm surprised at how rough she is, but it gets his attention. JR makes a sound like "Mmrrruhhh?" A few more small tugs and he's quiet. His eyes still flick over toward Greg, but his mouth is just hanging open.

"Come on over here," Mom says.

She's talking to me. She thinks I can help keep JR calm, but I'm not so sure. I am still technically a dude.

"Charming," says Greg, behind us.

"I've never seen that before," I say, not taking my eyes off JR. "I mean, he barks at me sometimes, but not like that."

"Like I said, he has a problem with adult males," says Mom.

"You think?" says Greg.

I reach JR and stand on the other side from Mom. He doesn't seem to mind, so I reach down slowly and scratch him behind the ear. He's calmer now.

"You can come on down," Mom says.

It makes me think of a game show. Greg takes the back steps slowly and then starts across the lawn. JR barks a few more times, but not like before. It seems like that storm has sort of passed.

"That's probably close enough," I say, just to be sure.

"You got him?" says Mom, loosening her grip.

She looks at me; I look down at JR; JR looks at Greg; Greg looks at us. It's like a four-way gunfight is about to break out.

"Sure," I say, digging my hand in under his collar. I can feel his neck muscles against my knuckles, and they're looser now, not as tensed up. "Got 'im."

Mom lets go and walks back toward Greg.

"So," says Greg, exhaling loudly, letting out some breath that's probably been in there for a while. "He's a rescue?"

"Yes," says Mom. "I got him from that big shelter just south of here."

"Yep," says Greg. He nods and JR follows the motion with his own head, up and down, like he's agreeing. Then he snaps off another bark, like he changed his mind.

"Shush, boy," I say, giving his collar a tug.

Greg's looking at him carefully, like he's trying to guess his weight. He's fully in lawyer mode now, and you can see he has mixed feelings about the rescue thing. I want to ask: What's wrong with being a rescue? But I'm not an idiot and I already sort of know. A rescue has had it bad; a rescue can be mean. But it's a good thing, too. You know, sympathetic. I'm sure Greg knows that. It cuts both ways. For a while, we're all looking down at JR and JR is looking up at us.

"What's his name again?" says Greg.

"Johnny," says Mom, choosing the friendliest option, the one that she uses.

"Hey, Johnny," says Greg.

JR cocks his head, closes his mouth, then lets it fall open again. He recognizes his name.

"Good dog," says Greg. I'm sure it's not the first time JR has been patronized. "And the, uh, incident, it was here in the backyard?"

"Yes," says Mom, unable or just not trying to prevent a sour-lemon expression from flashing across her face.

All of a sudden, my heart starts pounding. I need to tell him! I can tell him right now about Mars jumping the fence, cornering him. I can show him right where it happened. And Mom will vouch for me. This isn't court or anything, but I can still make, like, an official statement. I don't know why I'm so nervous about it, but I have to do it. It's the only thing I've got.

As all of these thoughts are rushing through my head, Greg slips something out of his pocket.

"Let me get the dog first," he says.

I panic for a second. "What do you mean, 'get the dog'?"

Greg holds up his digital camera, and I feel like an idiot.

"Could he move?" says Greg. "Could one of you move him over there? I want to get the tree in the background."

It's like picture day at school. JR doesn't understand what's going on, but between Mom and me, we don't have much trouble getting him into a more photogenic spot.

"Nice," says Greg as he takes the first picture.

JR blinks at the flash, then looks at the camera a little more closely, trying to figure out what just happened. Greg takes another shot.

"Even better," he says.

JR blinks again. He's much calmer now, but I can't tell if he's gotten used to Greg or has barked himself out.

"Is that, like, his mug shot?" I say.

"They already took that," says Greg. "But we can take our own, too. All ends up in the same place."

"Wait," I say. "They were here? Who was here? They took pictures?"

Greg lowers the camera and glances over at me. He looks a little surprised. Maybe he thought I knew already, or maybe he's deciding how much to tell me. His mouth isn't moving, though, so I look over at Mom.

"It doesn't matter," she says, but I don't buy that.

"When?" I say.

She shakes her head: It doesn't matter.

"Who?" I say. "Was it yesterday?"

I wasn't here, but someone had to let them in, so when? "Was it yesterday?" I repeat. She told me she found out right after I left. I assumed she meant a phone call, but now I'm thinking they came here. They came with their lawyer, hammering hard on the door and demanding to take pictures. If that's how it happened, they're lucky I wasn't here.

"It doesn't matter, Jimmer," she says. My name is a signal to drop it.

"But . . ." I say.

"It was yesterday," says Greg.

He's either saying that because it's true or to shut me up. I'm not sure what to say next anyway. But someone was here, in our house. Some lowlife, some parasite. And I'm sure they got JR all revved up and took pictures of him barking like a maniac.

"And where did it happen?" Greg asks, and that snaps me out of it.

Now I have to say it, and I'm angry anyway. I mean, where it happened is the whole thing. I think Mom even wants me to tell Greg, because she doesn't answer. Instead, she turns to me and says, "Jimmer?"

My lawyer, my uncle – my luncle – turns and looks at me. "Lay it on me," he says.

So I launch into it. "He claims he was still on the other side of the fence and our dog jumped up at him, right? Stuck his head over the top of it and bit him?"

"Yeah, that's basically –" Greg starts, but I don't really need confirmation. That's what Mars's mom told mine.

"Well, that's bull!" I say. "That's over there." I point to the side of the fence closest to us. "But he was over here." I point to the corner.

"Did you see him there?" says Greg. He has switched back to his neutral lawyer voice, which annoys me. He should be on our side!

"No," I say, "but that's where JR was, and he was freaked and wouldn't move for a long time."

"JR is the dog," Mom says to him. He nods.

"And," I say, loudly, to get his attention back. "And there was a fresh footprint right there." I point again.

"A footprint in the grass?" he says.

"A footprint in the dirt," I say. "Definitely his sneaker, too."

He looks down, but the dirt is flat and slick.

"Rainstorm," I say.

I can see him mulling it over.

"Yep," he says. "God's cleaning service."

His tone has changed again. Neutral lawyer is gone, replaced by folksy lawyer. I'm sure he's used that line on a jury more than once. I'm glad he's thinking along those lines.

"So that sucks," I say. "But I saw it."

"So you're saying he let himself in?" he says. "And then, what, back out again?"

"Yeah, he hopped the fence. He's been coming over for years, and for the last few of them, since he's been tall enough, he's always hopped it. So do I. It's easier. So, yeah, he hops the fence, backs JR into a corner, and sticks his hand in his face. JR isn't as freaked out by younger guys, but you see how excited he gets. You can't just . . . He's a rescue. . . ."

I still feel like I need to explain that last part, like why it doesn't have to be a bad thing, but Greg waves me off. "Right," he says, "and a big one. I understand."

"Dr. Sanderson says he's getting much better," Mom says. "Even right now he's so much better."

"And then he hopped back over," I say. "And that's when I saw him. But he already knew to watch out for the dog crap in the yard because he'd just been in here. See? See?!"

Something occurs to me and I rush over to the fence post closest to where Mars was standing. If he used his hurt hand to hop it on the way out, I figure there might still be some blood on the post. It's like *CSI: Stanton*. But there's nothing. God's stupid cleaning service. My luncle is watching me. He probably knows what I'm looking for, and he sees me not see it.

"Yeah," he says. "Provocation's tough to prove, regardless. He's come over before, and then there's the height of the fence to consider. . . . Let me get some more shots. We'll talk inside."

"But I totally saw it," I say.

"All right," he says, his voice more unreadable than ever. "We'll talk inside."

Greg is supposed to be on our side, but it feels like I just lost him.

"Do you still need him?" Mom says, meaning JR.

"No," he says.

"Come on, boy," I say. "Biscuit."

He looks up at me.

"Pizza roll," I add.

He follows Mom and me toward the door. Greg steps to the side and JR gives him one last look, one last bark.

"Watch your step," Mom repeats from the top of the steps.

Or don't, I think. Mom and JR head inside, but I stop in the doorway. Greg takes a few pictures of the fence: the spot where Mars claims JR jumped up at him. He lowers the camera and is about to put it in his pocket, but he raises it again and takes one quick shot of the corner where I found JR. He barely even aims, but I see the flash go off and I head into the house.

Mom and I are already waiting at the living room table by the time Greg comes inside. JR is over in his spot, still licking the biscuit off his lips and probably wondering where that pizza roll is. Greg takes a seat like he's sitting down to dinner. JR's head pops up and then disappears again, like a periscope. I think that's pretty good, considering the racket he made before.

"Well, hell," Greg says.

"Yep," Mom says.

"Yep," I say.

"Listen," he says to Mom. "There's something you should know. The former owner, the guy who had him before you —"

"The guy he was taken away from?" says Mom. She has a look of total disbelief on her face. Mine is just total confusion.

"Yep," says Greg. "Well, they got him to file a deposition."

"You're serious?" I say.

He looks at me in a way that makes it clear that he is. Now I understand where Mom's disbelief came from. The psychopath who kept JR chained to a tree, covered in ticks, has filed a deposition. Greg doesn't say what's on it, but he doesn't really need to. I can guess what it says already: dangerous dog, always biting, chained up to *protect the public.*

I push my chair back and stand up, but I don't have anywhere to go. They watch me as I sit back down. I bet that guy's just like Mars's family. I wouldn't be surprised if they're related, and I'm 1,000 percent sure they're promising him a cut of the money. Money we don't even have, but try telling them that. I bet all they see is my mom dressed up nice, coming from work or going to it.

"It's safe to say that this guy is 'not unknown to the court,'" says Greg. "But that deposition is still strike two."

Right, I think, because even the absolute worst people still count more than any dog. Mom must understand it, too, because she just nods.

"And you know they're asking for some significant damages," he says.

"For what? I gave him the frickin' bandages for free!"

Greg looks over at me.

"Bannnn-daaaaa-gessssss," I say, drawing it out. "It wasn't even that bad a bite."

I can tell that there's something else. I can see him deciding whether or not to clue me in. Mom calls Greg "maddeningly vague," and she's being nice.

"They're claiming possible nerve damage," he says.

"Wait, what?" I say.

"Which is either smart or true," he says.

"Neither one of those sounds like Mars," I say.

"Still and all," he says. "The complaint says a 'persistent tingling in his hand and wrist.' Or something like that. It's kind of the classic, because it's hard to prove but just about impossible to disprove."

And right there, I can see the genius of it. I wonder if it was Mars's idea or their lawyer's. Not for a second do I consider the possibility that it might be true. I could see using a line like that to get out of gym or something, but this is serious. This is real. I am so mad at Mars right now, I could tear him in half. This whole thing bites on so many levels.

"But –" I start. Suddenly, I have a million more things to say, like how Mars wouldn't look me in the eyes downtown and how there's no way that bite requires a sling, so if he's lying about that . . . But Greg raises his hand in a stop sign and says, "Doesn't matter."

I really wish people would stop saying that to me.

"End of the day," Greg says, "that boy was bitten, and they got someone else, even if it's not much of one, to say the dog's a biter. And he's a Rottweiler, which is, you know, one of those species: a 'bully breed.' Would be worse if he was a pit bull, but it would be a whole lot better if he was a Lab or something."

That doesn't seem fair. JR is afraid of his own shadow half the time. He's the opposite of a bully, so why should his breed matter? Mom starts to say something, but Greg gives her a stop sign, too. That makes me mad, because this is our house and she's my mom and this is all insane.

He takes a deep breath. "Bottom line," he says, and we lean in.

Right at that moment, I remember something. It's not like it is on TV. Greg doesn't think that way, and courtrooms don't operate that way. There's not going to be any high-tech crime-scene investigation or any dramatic last-second testimony. He just said it: That scumbag former owner filed a deposition, which means he's not even going to be there.

"We're going to go ahead and try to settle," he says. There it is. "They may not agree right away, may want to go to court. Or they might jump at it. It'll come down to the money, either way. This is the way to play it."

I lean back. This show is over.

"Good news and bad news," he says.

We let him choose.

"Good," he says. "Homeowner's insurance should cover most of it. I've been coordinating with the company, looked over your policy, and it's not too bad. Policy limit's a little low for this, but hopefully that won't matter."

Now it's Mom's turn to lean back. I know she was worried. I know she was thinking we'd lose the house. I was worried about that, too. "But the rates will go up, regardless," she says.

It's not a question, so Greg doesn't answer.

"Is that the bad news?" I say. I'm just hoping.

"Bad news," says Greg. "The judge will decide what to do with the dog."

"What do you mean, 'what to do'?" I say, but that's not really a question, either. He means whether to have him put to sleep, and I know this is my fault. It's my fault because Mars is my friend. Or he was.

"How can they just —" I say. I can't say it for some reason.

"Same as the money," Greg says, shrugging a little. "A dog's just property. I know you don't see it that way, but in the eyes of the court . . ."

I look away and Greg waits for me to look back. I guess he figures I need to hear this.

"If they agree he's dangerous, presents a threat to public safety . . . You want my advice," he says, "get yourself a new dog."

I don't want his advice.

"Maybe try something smaller this time. . . ."

"We already *have* a dog," I say.

"Take it out of the judge's hands," he says. "Show some responsibility. Might help."

Now he leans back. He might as well. He's laid it all on the table.

I look over at Mom. She looks serious. "I can't believe they're doing this," she says. "I've known them for ten years. I've always been . . ."

It seems amazing that I've known Mars for that long. I try to remember the first time he came over here, and come up with an image of him sitting in the front room, maybe first or second grade, fishing the last Dorito out of the bag.

Greg looks over to the far end of the room, where the top of JR's head is just visible. Mom and I both follow his eyes. Look at that, I want to say, he is already so much better with people — so much! I want to say that to Greg, but I don't. It's another one of those things that cuts both ways.

"Seems like a nice enough dog, and it's a nice thing you did, getting him from the shelter like that," says Greg. "Still, I think you need to seriously consider it."

Mom looks up. "I don't think that's something I can do," she says.

"Me neither," I say, not like anyone asked me.

Greg pushes his chair back and stands up. The last thing he says is: "Judge might do it for you, regardless. I am sorry."

It's not even noon when he leaves, but the day already feels like a total waste.

I turn to Mom: "Why did you say 'don't think' you can?"

She looks over at me, but her eyes are a million miles away.

"What's that?" she says.

"Unbelievable," I say and walk out.

28

I hear the car pull out of the driveway in the middle of the afternoon. Mom didn't even tell me where she's going, which is pretty unusual, but I guess it's that kind of day. Meanwhile, I've been lying like a lump in the front room for hours, half watching TV.

I still have three books I'm supposed to read before school starts. That's tomorrow, so that's pretty much not going to happen, but I figure I can power through one of them. I'm not going to get anything done lying on this couch, so I grab the thinnest book and head for the living room.

I sit in the chair closest to JR's spot, and he raises his head. I ask him where Mom went, but he's not saying.

"You're only fifty percent hers, you know," I say. "If you round down, that's zero."

He drops his head again, and I go back to my book. It's *Hiroshima* by John Hersey. I figured that was a metaphor, but, nope, it is actually about Hiroshima after the atomic bomb was dropped on it. I wonder if I made the wrong choice for a while, but it really is a short book and by then I'm already on page forty. I'm a pretty fast reader.

On page sixty-three, JR comes over and sits next to my chair. I don't know if he's leaving his spot or just expanding its edges a little. I reach down and sort of ruffle-scratch the fur between his ears. It's not something I would've tried even a few days ago, but I figure he didn't come over here to bite me and it turns out I'm right.

If someone were to walk by the living room window right now, well, 1) it would freak me out. They'd have to be standing in the backyard to be looking in. But 2) they'd just think they were looking at a normal kid and a normal dog. I'm doing my homework, and he's curled up next to my chair.

The rest of us are freaking out about the lawsuit, but JR doesn't really know what's going on, and I'm sort of hoping he never has to. Mom has been gone for a few hours now, and I let myself think — at least I let part of me think — that she'll take care of this. Maybe she's taking care of it right now, talking with Greg or whatever, just like she's always taken care of things for us.

By the time she gets back, JR is asleep and I've had enough of gruesome radiation burns and skin falling off and am ready for dinner. And sure enough, she comes back with a few bags of food and no explanation, as if buying forty bucks' worth of groceries took three and a half hours. This isn't one of those no-news-is-good-news situations, though. I figure if she's not telling me something, it's something I don't want to know. Plus, I'm hungry.

I head back to the front room after dinner, and when I walk past the clock, I realize I've got twelve hours until school starts up again. Between the people I'm not talking to, the ones who aren't talking to me, and the ones I haven't seen since the last time we were all there, tomorrow is going to be a total train wreck. I sit down on the couch, and the two books I didn't read are just looking at me. They're trying to blame me for passing them over, but I know it's their fault. Try being 160 pages, I want to tell them. Try being about nuclear destruction. Then we'll talk.

I watch some TV, but the books keep staring. This time they have a point. It's highly unlikely that I'm going to be tested on episode three of the *Seven Ages of Rock*. I reach over and pick up *Tess of the d'Urbervilles* by Thomas Hardy, but the thing is thick as a brick.

There's a knock on the side door, the one closest to where I am. I wait to make sure I'm not just hearing things. Whoever it is knocks again: one, two, three times. In case there was any doubt left, JR starts barking and I hear him heading down the hall. I get to the door a few steps before him and shield him off with my legs as I crack open the door. I am not at all prepared for who it is.

"Hey," I say.

"Hey," she says.

It's Janie. I can see her boxy little hybrid parked at the very end of the driveway, the back wheels practically in the road. Those things are quiet.

"I didn't, uh," I start. "I didn't expect."

It's not a full sentence, but it's close enough.

"You never do," she says. "But I thought, you know, you've humiliated yourself enough at this point."

"Yeah," I say. "That's probably true."

JR is working his way around, trying to stick his head out the open door, and I have to sort of hip-check him to keep his nose pinned against the door frame. He's built like a bulldozer and crazy strong.

"That your new dog?" she says, lifting her head up and to the side to get a better look.

"Nah," I say. "I have no idea who this is." I give him another little hip check and try to figure out how I'm going to let Janie in.

"I hear he bit Mars's arm off," she says.

"He should've."

29

"Sorry for the surprise," says Janie. "I won't be here long."

Things have calmed down now. JR stopped barking and went back into eek-a-person mode as soon as she made it in the door. He doesn't retreat back into the living room, though. He sticks around. It reminds me of that first night, when I fell and he barked at me, except this time, it's my legs he's hiding behind instead of Mom's.

Janie kneels down and holds her hand low to the ground, palm up. I'm not really sure what she's doing, but JR seems to know, because he takes a few steps toward her.

"You have to be careful with him," I say. "He's a rescue and —"

And then he makes a liar out of me by sniffing Janie's hand. She takes her time and lets him. Then, just like that, she brings her other hand up and pets him.

"He's not so bad," she says. She's looking at him when she says it and she draws the word *bad* out like baby talk for his benefit.

"I think it's mostly men he has a problem with," I say.

"I know how he feels," she says, standing up.

Walked right into that one. Mom ducks her head into the hallway just long enough to say hi to Janie. When Mom leaves, she takes JR back with her.

Once it's just Janie and me, the mood changes a little. The temperature drops, basically. She was friendly enough at the door, but it's pretty clear this is going to be a Serious Talk. I know I have it coming, but I hate these on principle. I sit down on the couch and I'm sort of hoping she will, too, but she sits in the creaky, old chair next to it.

"How's the garden store?" I say.

"Not too bad," she says. "Today was my last day. You're lucky you didn't catch me when you didn't."

"It take you all day to think of that?" I say.

"Actually," she says, "I thought of it while you were walking back across the parking lot."

"Yeah, I forgot something over there."

"What's that?" she asks.

"My pride."

"Don't joke," she says. I put my hands up like, OK, OK, but she started it.

"Did you mostly work inside, or outside with the plants and flowers and stuff?" I say.

"Little of both. It wasn't bad on nice days. Not exactly a dream job, but whatever."

"Yeah."

"So how was your summer?" she asks. I expected it, but somehow it still catches me off guard.

"Uh," I start, but she shoots me a look like: whatever comes out of your mouth better be the truth. So I shut my mouth again, because that way, at least it's not *not* the truth.

"Uh-huh," she says.

I'm about to try again, but I hear JR trotting back down the hall. I guess he slipped through Mom's defenses. I think he's going to come in and sort of let me off the hook, but all he does is poke his ginormous head in the room, look at us for a second, and then turn around and head back down the hallway.

"Just checking in," I say.

"I like your dog," she says.

"It's not true, you know. With Mars."

"I figured," she says.

"I mean, he did bite him, but Mars was a total dick and basically made him."

"Yeah," she says. "That sounds about right."

"And now he's making all kinds —"

"Listen!" she says, and I shut up. "We still need to talk, all right? Like, a real talk? And it's pretty clear that's still way too much to ask for, which is completely ridiculous, but whatever, I don't know what I even expected. We're back to school tomorrow, and people are going to be asking me what's going on, and I don't even know what to tell them. And that sucks."

It's all true, but I'm not sure which part to respond to first, or how. It amounts to me saying nothing for a little too long, which basically proves her point. She exhales in that let-down way, picks up *Tess of the d'Urbervilles*, and says, "You read it?"

I shake my head no.

"I read another one today," I say. *"Hiroshima."*

She makes a face, maybe because she didn't like the book or maybe just because it was so gruesome. I'm glad we have the same reading list, though. It means we've got the same English teacher. If we have him the same period, it could either be really good or a full year's worth of incredible awkwardness. I'm willing to take that chance.

"I found the movie on demand," I say. "I was thinking of watching it. . . ."

"Sounds like entertainment gold," she says.

She stands up, so I do, too.

"And anyway," she says, tossing the book back down on the table. "I've read it."

Of course she has. She's always been a better student than me.

"They give you the hybrid?" I say as she heads toward the door.

"Made me buy it for five hundred bucks," she says. "Paid them last month."

"That's a good deal," I say, like an idiot. "I always liked that car."

"Good," she says. "Then you can watch it drive away."

And I do. I stand there at the door, watch the headlights come on, and watch her back out and drive away. After that, I head back to the couch to order *Tess of the d'Urbervilles*. Turns out it's a miniseries — 240 minutes long! I make it through the first episode and half of the second — only two and a half to go — but I still have pretty much no idea what's going on. The actors are trying to out-British one another, and I was thinking about what Janie said the entire time.

I don't mind her taking a few shots at me like that. I deserve it, and if I could fix this just by taking enough abuse, it'd be no problem. I'm good at that. But I can't fix things that way. I've got to talk, like she said, really talk.

That's the problem. I'm not as good at that. I'm not good at it at all. But I have to try. I know that. I just don't know how.

30

I'm standing in the grass at the edge of my lawn, waiting for Rudy to pick me up for the first day of school. The bus has already come and gone, and I'm starting to think that maybe Rudy has forgotten about me. The only thing that's keeping me from being more upset about this is the fact that I'm half-asleep.

I stand perfectly still and listen. Rudy drives one of those cars that you can hear long before you can see it. It's a complete beater, an ancient hand-me-down Ford Fiesta that is somehow still on the road, an automotive zombie, the rolling dead.

A minute later, I hear it coming. It makes an irregular chugging sound, like one or more of its cylinders just isn't trying anymore. We tried to get it up to eighty on a flat, wide-open stretch outside town once and I thought it was literally going to explode. I turn and watch it round the corner and come into view. This is the official start of my junior year. Shoot me now.

Rudy is wearing his MUSTACHE RIDES 5 CENTS T-shirt. He doesn't have a mustache, and may not be capable of one, but it's one of the few T-shirts he has that won't automatically land him in detention. A button-up shirt that probably covered it when he left his house is crumpled up next to him. We exchange greetings in a slurry of mumbles, but by the time we reach the parking lot, we're both wide awake. It's like a fight-or-flight thing, and our adrenaline has kicked in. He finds a spot and we climb out. Two rows up, I see Aaron's Malibu. We hustle in, already borderline late.

Solomon T. Dahlimer High School. I recognize it by the smell. We mostly call it Dahlimer, but the thing to do at football games is chant, *"S-T-D! S-T-D!"* Anyway, the first few periods are a blur of little adjustments: new schedules and classes, repainted hallways, and students who are either new or significantly changed.

I see Mars a few times but it's at a distance each time, and neither of us makes any effort to close it. He's a level down and not in any of my classes. He's not wearing his sling, but his hand is wrapped in so many layers of gauze and white tape, it looks like a polar bear paw. I see Aaron up close, but we don't say more than a few words to each other the first time and mostly just nod after that. It's early, and we've all got other things to think about.

It's not until lunch that the day really slows down and comes into focus.

"I am *not* sitting with frickin' Mars," I say to Rudy as we head down the long back hallway that leads to the cafeteria.

"Aw, you're kidding me," he says.

"Dude, he's *suing* my *mom*."

"OK, OK," he says.

We both start scoping out the hallway, because now we have to avoid sitting alone, or worse. We both know who we're looking for, and we see a group of them in a side hallway outside the caf.

We call them the Goonies. They're not exactly our friends but sometimes we hang out with them at school, sit with them at lunch, that sort of thing. It's not that we don't get along with them; it's just that we don't feel the need to do more than that. I'm pretty sure they feel the same way about us. It's more like an alliance, I guess.

Randall, Jesse, and Tal — all Goonies — are talking to a kid I don't know. He's new and clearly a prospective Goonie. We head over to them.

"S'up, losers," says Rudy.

"Ladies," I say, gesturing toward the group.

I say it like I mean it, because our number one job is to keep the stink of desperation from settling on us. If they realize we need to sit with them, they'll lord it over us and piss on us the whole time.

"Hey, what a coincidence," says Jesse. "We were just telling Evan here that this school has a top-notch special ed program."

Rudy and I flip him off with a synchronized precision that impresses even us. Then we settle in and listen as they return to their regularly scheduled conversation. When it's over, we all head to the caf together. The conversation is easy after that. All we have to do is complain about the food and express profound disbelief that we're back here again.

I scan the room as we find a spot. Mars is sitting with Aaron at a packed table near the windows. Mars sees me look over, checks who I'm with, and smirks. He raises his "injured" hand and waves. I raise my healthy one and flip him off. That particular muscle gets a lot of work on the first day of school. Really, you should start conditioning it the week before. Aaron watches us. I see the flash of blue as he flicks his eyes in this direction. You can always tell when he's looking; you just can't tell what he's thinking. The Goonies watch, too.

"Heard your dog bit Mars," says Tal.

"He's full of crap," I say.

"I didn't say he tasted good," says Tal. "But is it true?"

"Kind of," I say, shrugging.

I can see them all processing the information, trying to figure out what it means for the social landscape of our class. Is this just a feud between Mars and me, or is it more than that? All except for the new kid, Evan, who doesn't know any of the people involved and knows better than to try to play catch-up. That's smart. It's pretty clear that if he doesn't end up a Goonie, it'll be because he turns them down, not vice versa.

I keep tabs on Mars the whole time. I need to come up with some sort of strategy, something more productive than this low-boil hostility. Toward the end of lunch, I see him reach into his backpack and take out his sling. It's still by far the cleanest, whitest thing he owns, and he starts putting it on right there. Why? I try to think along with him. It's not that hard; he's not that complicated. He must have gym next.

I ask myself, What will he do now? And then I know that, too. At the end of lunch, Rudy and I are dumping out our trays and I say, "Catch you later."

"Sure," he says, and I think he's relieved to get a break from feud duty.

Then I head to the men's room in between the caf and the gym and wait. It requires some pretend hand washing and pawing through my backpack, just to avoid any suspicion that I'm in there to check out the dudes. I don't have to wait long, though. Even better, the place is empty when Mars arrives.

31

Mars probably registers that someone else is in the room, but he doesn't look over, so he doesn't realize it's me. He stands in front of the metal mirror, adjusting his sling, getting it ready for show-time. I step in front of the door and lean back against it. Mars is crazier than me, but I'm bigger.

"Take that stupid thing off," I say, and he jumps about three feet straight up.

"Oh, hey, man," he says once he lands. He's trying to look calm, and he actually gives the mirror a quick sideways glance to see how he's doing.

"Take it off, man," I say.

"You say that in here a lot?" he says.

I take a step forward.

"I need it!" he says, taking a step back.

"For what?" I say.

A small smile flashes across his face. He licks his lips and it's gone. "To get out of gym," he says.

"Yeah, and for court," I say. "This isn't some joke, man. This is serious. This could be really bad."

"Should've thought of that before," he says. "I've got nerve damage."

"You've got brain damage."

Someone starts to push the door. I wait for it to get about a foot open, then mule-kick it closed.

"Ow!" I hear as it slams behind me. "What the —"

"Occupied!" I shout without turning around.

I wait a few beats, but the door stays closed. The timing is actually pretty good; Mars looks a little freaked. I've got his attention now. For a few seconds, we just stare at each other. He has a red scab under his left eye from a pimple he must've tried to pop too soon. I wonder which hand he used. Then, kind of pathetically, he says, "I've gotta get to gym."

"Not with that —" I start, but I reconsider. I'd dearly love to pound some sense into Mars right now, but it wouldn't solve anything: He's sense-proof and would just show up tomorrow in a fake body cast. I take a breath and my nose fills with the rank smell of the boys' room. I remind myself: strategy, not hostility. I start again.

"Listen, man," I say.

This is the second time I've tried this sort of changeup on Mars and he recognizes it immediately. His shoulders relax and his mouth turns up in half a smirk. He remembers that, cornered or not, he's in the driver's seat here.

"Yeah?" he says.

"You gotta let this drop," I say.

"Not my call," he says. "They haven't asked me once."

An honest answer is the last thing I expect from Mars right now, and I have no idea how to respond. He goes on.

"My whole thing is just to be injured," he says. "It's, like, my job. Mom's job is doing the law stuff, the lawyer."

It's funny how, no matter what is going on, your brain can't help identifying a potential joke. Seriously, you could be at a funeral and the priest could set one up, and everyone would be standing there, dressed in black and thinking it. I go ahead and say it.

"Your mom is doing the lawyer?"

"Phhh," he says.

"I'm serious, man," I say. "My mom doesn't make that much money. Just keeping the house is killing her. And the judge, he could have JR put to sleep. Which is lame."

"Yeah, what has he ever done for me except bite me?" he says. "Maybe he is dangerous?"

It comes out as a question. He's hoping it's true.

"He's not. He just doesn't like to be cornered."

• "Yeah, well, I don't, either," says Mars. He has a point.

The door starts to open behind me again. I think Mars will use the opportunity to push past me, but he just stands there. We both turn to see who it is. I don't recognize him, and he's really scrawny. Put those two things together and he's a freshman, a nobody. He stands there, just inside the door. He can tell something's going on.

"Hey," he says.

Neither of us answers. He turns around and leaves. It's the first day of school, and we're the guys his mother warned him about.

I turn back toward Mars. We're both going to be late now. We'll both end up using the same excuse: new schedule, got confused.

"But you can talk to your mom," I say. "Or talk to your dad."

"Yeah, right," he says.

"You don't have to go along with, you know, the 'nerve damage,'" I say.

I stop there. I saw him put on the sling at lunch; I saw him without it all day. I know he's lying, just like I know he's lying about how it happened. I'm just not sure it'll help to say so. We're alone here in this little room that smells like piss, but Mars is being way more honest than I expected.

"I suppose I could make a dramatic recovery," he says.

"Yeah!" I say, a little too fast.

Mars looks to both sides, as if he has to double-check that no one else is in here.

"But why should I?" he says.

"Because," I start. I really should've had an answer ready for that one. "Because you should. It's, you know."

I can't stand here and say, "It's the right thing to do," to Mars. Who am I, Captain America?

"If we get all that money, I'll get at least some," he says. "Which is more than I've got now."

"All what money?" I say. "We don't have —"

"You give me something," he says, cutting me off.

"What?"

"Something."

"I don't have," I say. "I have, like, nothing. Basically."

Out in the hall, the bell goes off.

"You have information," he says.

"About what?" I say. "Oh."

"Yeah," he says. "You're finally going to tell me."

I don't bother with any of my standard denials, just like he didn't bother with any of his. I breathe in. The truth – it really does smell like crap sometimes.

"You really want to know that bad?"

"Sure," he says. "I mean, we've known each other for forever, man. This is, like, the first thing I don't really know about you, and that kind of bothers me. And we're friends, right? We're supposed to be, and so maybe I don't feel too good about this, either. But you've got to give me something. Even if I don't really want to go through with all this anyway, I still need something for it."

It sounds almost reasonable when he puts it that way, like a favor between friends or, what do they call that, a good-faith gesture? I want to believe him.

"But you can't tell anyone," I say.

"Aaron," he says.

"Other than that," I say. "And then you'll, like, drop it?"

"Then I'll see what I can do," he says, spreading his hands in front of him like a movie mobster, cutting a deal.

Dammit. I might have to do this.

"But no more bull," he says. "The truth, all of it, for real."

"Course," I say.

"So?" he says.

"Not now," I say, just stalling. "You've got to get to gym."

"Yeah, right," he says. "When, then?"

I look at him. I have to do this. But there's something else I have to do first.

"Tomorrow morning, before homeroom."

32

I'm in kind of a daze by the last class of the day, even more than usual. It's English. I look around for familiar faces and get a seat next to Rudy, on the far side of Aaron. Janie's in the front, not looking at me. I have a good view of the back of her head and her neck. If we keep these seats all year, it's going to end up driving me insane. I try to think of something else.

"You read any of the books?" I ask Rudy.

He sits up straight, pushes a finger along the bridge of his nose like he's adjusting a pair of glasses, and says, "I did extensive research online."

He read the summaries on Wikipedia. I let out a quick laugh.

Aaron looks over. "What?"

I let Rudy answer. "Nothing," he says. "It's stupid."

"Yeah, speaking of stupid," says Aaron. "What were you doing with the Goonies today?"

Rudy points to me, as if that explains everything. Aaron looks me in the eyes. "Yeah," he says. "You two need to get that fixed."

"What?" I say. As if this was just some misunderstanding or something. It's just like him to grade Mars on a curve like that.

Still, getting it fixed is exactly what I'm trying to do. Maybe he already knows.

"You heard me," says Aaron.

I let it drop. Getting into it with him is a bad idea. If I tell Mars, it's the same as telling Aaron. At least Mars was upfront about that, but how do I know that's as far as it would go?

Class starts and Mr. Kibbee writes the name of our first book on the dry-erase board with a bright red marker. It's from our reading list: Guess which one. If you bet one hundred dollars that it isn't the one I'd read and then doubled down that it isn't the one whose miniseries I just started, then congratulations. You are now rich.

This book is called *Things Fall Apart*. . . . Tell me about it. People start going through their bags for their copies. Not me, I wasn't going to bring all three just to see which one he picked first.

All around me, my classmates are getting a head start on what promises to be a full year's worth of diligent brownnosing. "This was intense!" says Edgar, dropping the book on his desk. "Seriously!" says Jason, pulling his copy out of his backpack like he's producing a rabbit out of a hat.

Janie turns and looks at me. She knows I didn't read this one, and since it was on the list, we won't be given any time to now. We'll just go straight into discussing it, and I'll go straight into keeping my hand down and avoiding Kibbee's eyes. She makes her eyes wide with fake surprise, like: Wow, a book from our summer reading list. Who would've thought?

She's kind of being a jerk, but all I can think is how good she looks. Her eyes look lighter against her summer tan. I nod, conceding defeat, and she turns back around.

The rest of class goes as slowly as you'd expect, but eventually it crawls across the finish line. The first day of school is in the books, even if I haven't read them, and Rudy and I are heading toward the student parking lot. He's talking rapid fire about which girls are in which of his classes. Amanda Lehane is in two of them and may or may not have gotten breast implants.

"I say yes," he says. "What do you think?"

"Yeah, probably," I say. "I mean, the change is pretty noticeable."

"I guess it could just be, like, some very strategic growth."

"Yeah, but that's a little too strategic. What did she do, make a wish when she blew out her birthday candles?"

"Wish she'd blow out my birthday candle," he says.

As we push through the double doors, I see Aaron's car roll through the stop sign at the edge of the lot and accelerate smoothly up the hill toward the traffic light.

"– cost?" says Rudy.

"What?" I say. I missed the question.

"Are they expensive?" he says. "Boob jobs?"

"I think it depends," I say.

It's not much of an answer, but I'm about 100 percent distracted. If I'm going to tell Mars (maybe) and he'll tell Aaron (obviously) and neither of them can be completely trusted (probably), then I've got to tell Rudy first.

This all sucks. I don't like being backed into a corner any more than JR does. But Rudy can't hear it secondhand. I owe him that. Well, more than that, but that'll have to do. "Hey, man," I say. "Can we, like, take the long way back, like Mill Pond maybe?"

"Sure, if the car doesn't die," he says. "What's up?"

33

Rudy's tiny Ford is older than we are. It was built in 1993 and not even all that well. We are chugging along Burnside Road, listening to the engine slowly give up on this world, and not saying anything. It's a little awkward. Rudy's my best friend and the most inappropriate person I know, so you'd think I could talk to him about anything. I used to think that, too, but this one has had me stumped for months.

"So," he says finally. "What're we, checking out the sights? Leaf peeping?"

"No," I say. I'm trying to figure out how to start, how or if.

We get stuck behind one of those little post office trucks with the steering wheel on the wrong side. When the guy pulls over to stick a handful of catalogs and bills in the next mailbox, Rudy pulls out into the other lane. The Fiesta labors past and then backfires at its vanquished opponent.

With the road open in front of us, Rudy tries again: "Nice day for a drive, huh?"

I'm ready to talk now.

"You know how, like in cartoons, the first assignment kids always get at the start of school is an essay?" I say.

"Maybe," says Rudy. "What kind of essay?"

"What I did on my summer vacation."

"Oh," he says. "Oh yeah."

"Well," I say.

"I was not expecting this. Not at all."

"I'm a man of mystery."

"You're a tight-lipped ass."

"That's a badly mixed metaphor."

"Stay on target," he says. He knows my tricks. "What you did on your summer vacation. About time, by the way. About time you told me."

"Well," I say. "I didn't spend it with my aunt."

"Knew it!" he shouts. "Man, you lie like a rug. Now tell me where you really were, so I can decide how pissed to be right now."

"I really was upstate," I say. "That part was true."

"Congratulations."

"I was in, well, I was in juvie. It was one of those big, half-empty places upstate."

"Was it like, what, a prison?"

"It was half like that, and half like, I don't know, kindergarten," I say. "They just treated us like potentially dangerous children. Which I guess we kind of are, but still. We had to talk about our 'feelings' a lot, and you know how much I like that."

"Right, like: 'And how did that make you feel?'" he says.

"Exactly."

"OK, so why were you there?"

"Yeah," I say. "That's the thing. It's just . . . it's not good."

"Yeah, I figured there was some reason you were stonewalling. I mean, juvie . . . It's almost kind of cool."

"It's not cool! That's just stupid. That's just, whatever, it's ridiculous. People who say that haven't been there, like it makes you some kind of badass. It makes you a loser, all right? First of all —"

"Whoa, I just meant —" Rudy says, but I'm not done.

"First, it's the most depressing place on Earth. And that's in the summer. In the winter, I don't even know. Second, what do I need that for? Who am I going to impress? How hard is it to be tough around here anyway? It's not. People already think we're at least that. What do I need the extra credit for? And you know what I don't need? I don't need everyone knowing and just putting that on me. I don't want to be a dead-end loser. I am going to frickin' get out of here and not hang around downtown at, like, twenty-seven, trying to save up for smokes, all right?"

"Jesus," says Rudy. "Relax, all right? I'm not going to put it on your permanent record."

I sit back and breathe. It doesn't seem like enough, so I pop my head out the open window and let the air blast my face for a few seconds. When I duck back in, Rudy asks the same question: "Why?"

It's possible that my entire speech was some kind of attempt to avoid answering him the first time. It's possible he knows it.

"You can't tell anyone," I say.

This is the part I never wanted to admit, the part I wanted to just bury in a hole for the rest of my life. But there's no avoiding it now: I can't tell the what without the why. I can't believe I'm going to do this. I'm disgusted with myself.

"I stole perfume," I say.

It's quiet for a few seconds — or as quiet as a mistreated 1993 Ford Fiesta can be — as Rudy tries to decide whether or not I'm joking. A few seconds stretch to a few more. Then Rudy says something equally crazy.

"I gotta say, when you, like, *asked us here today,* for this long, slow drive through the frickin' woods, I thought: Oh Christ, he's gonna tell me he's gay. And then I was relieved it was something else, but now I'm like: 'Wait, are you? Is that what this is?'"

"What? Shut the hell up!" I say. I'm pretty sure he's just saying that to cut the tension, but I'm not 100 percent sure. "See, that's why I didn't want to even . . . Christ."

"But, dude, you stole *perfume*?"

"It was for my mom! For Mother's Day," I say. "I wanted to get her something nice 'cause, whatever, her year has kind of sucked, and I haven't exactly helped."

"Well, that's . . . I mean, I can see that. But, I mean . . ."

"Yeah, believe me, I know. It's bad. I went into that place downtown. That stupid little . . ." I can't bring myself to say "boutique," but there aren't that many possibilities downtown and Rudy figures it out.

"Illusions?"

"That's the place."

"Never been in there."

"I hadn't either, but it seemed worth a shot. So I was looking around and everything basically cost more than I had. The lady was watching me really closely, but then I told her why I was there — looking for a gift for my mom — and she calmed down.

And she just, I don't know, calmed down too much. She went in the back to check on something, and I pocketed it."

"The perfume?"

"Yeah."

"And you left?"

"Yeah."

"So how did they . . . ?"

"Hidden cameras, like, three of 'em," I say.

"I guess that explains the calmness," he says.

"Yeah, I didn't even check. It just didn't seem like a high-security environment."

"So, wait, they sent you to juvie for stealing perfume? Did you, like, punch her to get away? Or wait, was it because of the fight?"

"Kind of. They definitely brought it up."

"That's lame. We wouldn't even have gotten in trouble for that if we hadn't won so bad."

"That's all on Aaron. I was pretty much useless."

"Showed you can take a punch."

"Or eight. Anyway, it was mostly the perfume. It was really expensive. They were like, 'That's our best perfume!' Which it probably was, but I mean, that was kind of the point."

"Like how much?"

"Like, two hundred bucks."

"No way!"

"Yeah, which is also apparently the difference between petty theft and theft in this state. It actually could've been worse. My uncle is a really good lawyer, at least at that kind of stuff. He's been useless with Mars, but he struck a deal super quick so I could serve the time over the summer. The whole summer."

"Damn," says Rudy.

"Yeah."

"So you spent the summer in a high-security kindergarten upstate for stealing perfume?"

"Yeah."

"But you're not gay?"

"Drop dead."

"Remember how I said it was kind of cool before?"

"Yeah."

"Well, I take it back. Obviously."

"Obviously."

"Damn."

"You can't tell anyone," I say. "Ever."

"Course not," he says, and he might even mean it. He leans back in his seat and looks around at the world, like it changed somehow while we were talking. In a way, it did. Just the fact that someone else knows now, the fact that it's out there, even if it never goes any further, it changes things. It knocks me down several dozen pegs, for one thing. I might as well finish the job.

"It's like you try and be who you want to be, and listen to the music you like instead of what everyone else is listening to, and not take crap from people and act in a way that lets them know not to give you any," I say, looking straight ahead out the windshield. "And then the world comes along and pulls your frickin' pants down."

"Yeah," says Rudy. "You got pantsed. And spritzed."

"Yeah, ha-ha. But you see why I didn't tell you?"

"Kind of," he says. "Still should've told me. Kind of dickish not to. You don't think I knew you were full of it? You don't think I wanted to know?"

I think back to that day at Wendy's, the sneak attack. "No, I knew. I was just . . . kind of dickish."

"Yep."

He takes the turnoff at Mill Pond Road. As he's straightening out the wheel, he adds: "Just don't tell Mars."

I don't answer.

34

Rudy pulls the Fiesta up along the grass in front of my house. He keeps the engine running because starting it is sometimes an issue.

All I can think to say is: "Well then."

"Yep," he says.

We've already said enough. He manages a quick, strained smile, and I climb out of the car. The Fiesta sputters a few times but doesn't quite stall, and it picks up speed as it drives away. I walk across the lawn in pretty much the same way. Rudy was actually super cool about it, much cooler than I thought.

It's kind of weird to think of your best friend having something like that over you. Not that I think he'd ever use it. How many embarrassing things do we know about each other by now? But then it's weird to think of keeping something like that from your best friend for months, of either lying to him or avoiding the topic.

I'm not second-guessing that. I know why I did it: It's embarrassing as hell, and I really did want to bury it forever. I bet everyone has at least one thing they're taking with them to the grave – some bad thing they did or thought. It seemed like this could've been mine, if I could've waited them out, or if they just would've let it drop. Frickin' Mars, man.

JR's face pops into view in the window of the kitchen door. He's looking straight at me with eyes so round and wide that it's like he's trying to hypnotize me. Maybe he is. *You are getting sleepy. . . . You are getting me biscuits. . . . You are letting me out the back door before something bad happens. . . .*

As I reach the door, he starts whacking the glass with his paws, like phantom high fives. I open it quick before he breaks anything and remember at the last second to wedge my body into the gap before he can squeeze past.

He gives ground as I enter the kitchen, and before I can even close the door, he's shooting through the house, heading for the back door. As I swing the door closed behind me, I see something blue hanging off the inside doorknob.

I make a mental note of my own to come back and take a look after I let JR out. He clearly has some pressing needs right now. I open the back door and he launches himself out into the yard. I leave it open so he can come back in on his own and head back to the kitchen.

The thing on the doorknob is just a few nylon straps, circles and lines connected by a couple of metal rings. There's a Post-it note stuck to the door next to this thing and I lean down to read it. The note says: *Put this on if you walk him!*

It's a frickin' muzzle. It's a bad idea in so many ways. One, I'm not really sure he'd let me put it on him; two, he'd hate it; and three, what do you think when you see a dog with a muzzle on? You think he's dangerous. You think he has to wear it or he'll bite.

It reminds me of *The Silence of the Lambs*, one of those movies that's always on some channel late at night, the scene where they put the mask on Hannibal Lecter. And it's not true, either – well, it is for Hannibal, but not for JR. People just have to not be stupid around him and he's fine.

I crumple up the Post-it and let the muzzle drop back against the door. I turn around and JR is right there. I jump like eight feet. It's not because of him: I'm still thinking of *Silence of the Lambs*.

"Scared me, boy," I say.

I sort of wonder what he's doing back so soon and why he's standing here, but I think I know. I turn around and look at the window on the kitchen door again. There are nose prints on it, and not just the ones from when I got home. He's been looking out the window all day.

"You missed me, huh?"

Apart from that one trip to Brantley last week, this is the first time we haven't spent the day together, at least in the same house. I look down at him and he looks up at me. And then it's like: What the heck, I've already said so many embarrassing things today, what's one more?

"Missed you, too," I say.

JR doesn't say anything, just stands there, waiting for his biscuit.

35

Back in the dark ages, before cell phones, a guy could probably call a girl, change his mind before she picked up, and not have her call him back three seconds later. That time has past. My phone is on vibrate, skittering spastically across the tabletop. The name on the screen is JANIE.

I pick it up, put it down, pick it up again, and answer: "Hey."

"What, you hung up on me?" she says.

"Dropped call," I say.

"Bull," she says.

I try again: "False start."

"Better than an early finish," she says.

"That was one time!"

And now the conversation has officially begun. I guess it had to. Janie is the other person who absolutely can't find out about this secondhand. She would straight up de-ball me. JR seems to be taking that OK, but I don't think I could make the adjustment.

I take a deep breath. "You know that essay that kids write on the first day of school, like in cartoons and stuff?"

It's easier to tell her. It surprises me how much easier it is. Part of it is that I just told Rudy, and I'm recycling large chunks of material, and then I remember the rest. The other part is that I already had this conversation with her, even if it was just in my head.

It was last May, I guess. Janie had just gotten her license and I'd just been sentenced. I'd spent the day before waiting around the courthouse with Mom and Greg, and then we were in and out in what felt like no time at all. Greg had already made the deal, so I just went in there to hear the judge talk at me and bang her little wooden hammer, and that was that: summer upstate.

I spent a lot of the next twenty hours thinking about how I was going to tell Janie, and then I spent all of the hours after that not telling her. It was too perfect a day. And when I didn't do it that night, I started to get the stupid idea that maybe I could keep it all a secret, that I could just do the time and come back and it would be like it never happened.

So I've told her pretty much the whole story at this point. "And I already had that other thing," I say, tacking it on at the end so that maybe she won't notice. But she does.

"That stupid fight?" she says. "With those skaters?"

"Yeah," I say. I don't bother with my standard excuses — how one of them threw the first punch, and I should know because I took it — she's heard them before. "But we basically just got a warning for that."

"So this was your second time?" she says.

"Kind of," I say, "and I took something that was really expensive, so it was worse."

I get another crazy stupid idea: I'm just going to tell her the truth on everything. Because I need to try harder with her. I need to be better, and maybe this can be how I start. I feel like I have a chance, because she's still listening and not hanging up.

"Idiot," she says. "So what was it? What'd you take that was so expensive?"

"Perfume," I say, crazily, stupidly.

"What kind?" she says.

Now there's something Rudy didn't ask. I try to remember.

"SaFire, I think. It's misspelled, like Adventure Tyme."

That's where we went that day: Adventure Tyme Amusement Park, a small park on a lake about fifty miles from here. She drove, her first real trip as a licensed driver. I'm not sure why they spell *Tyme* that way; I guess maybe it's supposed to seem old-fashioned. Which doesn't explain the roller coasters and laser tag. Whatever the reason, we started calling it Adventer Tyme Abusement Pork, and it seemed like the funniest thing in the world. Of course, everything seems funnier when you're at an Abusement Pork on a sunny day with a licensed driver who is, to me, still the most beautiful girl I've ever seen and she's wearing a tank top.

"That's not fair," she says.

She means it's not fair to bring that memory up in this conversation. And she's right, but it's what I was thinking and I'm being honest today. There was this game we played toward the end of the day. It's hard to describe, but it was basically a big Plexiglas case with a bunch of moving shelves inside. The shelves had hundreds of quarters piled on them, and all you did was drop another quarter into one of the slots and watch it land inside. But the shelves were already piled so high and moving back and forth, so sometimes that one quarter would be enough to cause a bunch of other quarters to spill over the edge. Then you reached in the bottom and pulled them out.

Of course, most of the time you just lost a quarter, but we got lucky. It was maybe the third or fourth quarter we dropped. We'd just broken a dollar. Right before I put it in, Janie said, "Like a wishing well, like making a wish." And so I did. I think she did, too. Then I dropped the quarter and it was like a little silver landslide. We both reached in to scoop out our little haul and we split it. The day I left for upstate, my pockets were still half full of quarters. I knew they'd just take them away when I got there, but I had to bring them. It seemed like the wish wouldn't come true otherwise. As it turned out, it didn't anyway.

So now I'm done telling Janie, and the phone is so quiet that I think maybe she hung up. I've stopped pacing, and now I'm just standing there holding the phone to my ear. I'm waiting for her to tell me never to talk to her again — she honestly deserves better than a juvenile delinquent who lied to her and still doesn't have his license — or for her to tell me something else. Instead, she asks a question. "Why now?" she says. "Why are you telling me this now?"

The thing about crazy, stupid decisions, whether you decide not to tell anyone anything or to tell one person everything, is this: They give you a real sense of freedom. I've already made up my mind, so now I open my mouth. I tell her about Mars. I tell her, even though it will probably piss her off that the only reason I'm finally telling her all this is that I've basically been forced to.

"You two deserve each other," she says when I finish.

"Probably," I say. "But my mom deserves better. So does my dog."

"So do I," she says. "I have this whole time."

I can't argue with that, so I don't.

"But do you think he'll actually do it?" she says. "Call it off, I mean. Do you think he even can?"

She's just saying what I've been thinking this whole time. But it's the only move I've got, so I've got to try. It's like dropping a single quarter into that game: There's a chance if you do and no chance if you don't. I don't tell her that, though. That definitely wouldn't be fair.

"Guess I'll find out," I say, but she's already hung up.

36

Rudy leaves me hanging Tuesday morning. The grass is still wet from some overnight rain and my sneakers are soaked through by the time I wake up enough to realize what's happened. I know I deserve it, but it's still a major pain in the butt. The bus has already come and gone and I have to scramble to get a ride from Mom. Now she's going to be late, but I have to do it; I'm supposed to meet Mars before homeroom.

"Miscommunication," I say to Mom, and she doesn't ask again, just takes a long sip of coffee from her travel mug every few minutes. Her car is less of a beater than the Fiesta, so we make good time.

Rudy acts like nothing happened when we bump into each other in the hallway. I do, too. Sometimes you just have to take the hit. Speaking of which, "Got to go make Mars's day," I say to Rudy.

"You going to tell him?"

"Kind of have to," I say, leaving it at that.

"Your funeral."

It's not hard to find Mars. He's digging through his locker for something, already a huge mess in there after exactly one day. I stand against the wall on the other side, so that when he slams his locker shut, there I am. He jumps.

"Jesus, JD," he says, and then he remembers why I'm there and his eyes light up. It's like watching a thick morning fog burn off in half a second, and it gives me kind of a sick feeling. After telling Rudy and Janie, telling Mars should be easy. Should be, but I can tell immediately that it won't be. I feel defensive, nervous. I don't trust him the way I trust those two.

"Let's walk," he says.

We're headed around the corner, to a quieter hallway with no lockers. We're ten feet in and the sound behind us has already faded to a dull roar. Mars turns around, looks at me, and says, "So?"

This is stupid, I think, and it seems so true that I consider saying it. But the idea of this all just going away is really strong. "All right," I say, but I'm still trying to convince myself. I remember what he said yesterday, the one line that hooked me: "We're friends, right?" It's not that I even necessarily doubt him on that. We've definitely known each other long enough. It's just that he was never that reliable of a friend.

"Come on, Jimbo," says Mars. "Lay it on me."

"Have you talked to your mom?" I say. "Your dad?"

"I will," he says. "I was scouting out the terrain last night."

A teacher walks by. She doesn't know who we are, not by name anyway, but she gives us a long look the whole way. We act like we're talking about nothing, and then she passes and I tell Mars everything, more or less. I tell him I got caught shoplifting downtown. I remind him about the fight, not that he'd forget. None of us was exactly blameless in the lead-up to it, but he's the one who started shouting back at them. I'm not trying to put that whole thing on him. I'm just giving him something else to think about.

Then I tell him about upstate and rattle off a lot of details fast. I'm hoping there's only so much information he can process at this hour. I think it's even working because he wants to know all about that part. "How much like prison is it?" he says. "Like prison on TV?"

"Well, it lasts a lot longer than an hour, for one," I say.

He thinks that's funny, and I add some more. I tell him how the place where I was had kind of like a halfway house vibe, how they called it a "treatment program," "rehabilitation." He makes a don't-drop-the-soap joke and seems really disappointed when I tell him it wasn't like that, either. I shouldn't have said that. I feel like I need to give him his money's worth, humiliation-wise.

I'm talking and talking, and it's like that nightmare where you're running down a hallway but never getting closer to the end. The idea of him having his folks drop the lawsuit is the door I'm trying to get to, but the look on his face, the tone of his voice, none of it's changing. And then I'm done, and the bell's about to go off anyway. It's not the first day of school anymore, and if we're late, we're really late.

"Man," he says. "You're like a felon or something."

I shrug, acting embarrassed. He needs to think there's some reason I haven't told him this already. But he sniffs it out.

"So that's it?"

"Yeah," I say.

"Wait," he says. "What'd'ya take?"

The warning bell goes off and it occurs to me I haven't even been to my own locker yet. That door at the end of the hallway is even farther away now, so I reach for it. I grab the handle.

"But you seriously can't tell anyone," I say.

"Course, man," he says.

"Perfume," I say, "for Mother's Day. Really expensive perfume."

He erupts into laughter. Mars laughs like a hyena when he thinks something is really funny. It's not one of his better qualities, and most of his other qualities aren't that good.

"That's enough, man," I say.

He holds up his hand, like, I'm trying. The final bell's about to go off and I leave him there, still laughing. The last words I say to him are: "We have a deal!"

We do, and I've definitely done my part. The hallway from the nightmare vanishes, and now I'm running down a real one.

I try to feel good about it, like I've crossed some tough job off my to-do list. The next time I see Mars, he's stopped laughing and gives me a serious-looking thumbs-up. I even start to think that maybe Rudy and I should sit at the table with him and Aaron at lunch, but in between second and third periods, I find out how wrong I am. How wrong, and how stupid.

A junior named Travis and a sophomore whose name I forget are heading toward me in the hallway. Travis is a level down from me, which means he's in most of the same classes as Mars.

He takes a big whiff of the air as we pass. "Smells nice," he says. His voice is trailing off now, and the sophomore is chuckling like the little toady he is, so I barely hear the rest. "Almost like perfume."

I whip my head around, but all I manage to do is stare.

Two seconds later, Rudy rounds the corner.

"Dude," he says.

"I just heard."

37

The rest of the morning goes about how you'd expect: like a war movie. I track down Mars in the same way a heat-seeking missile tracks down a jet. He's by his locker when I find him, and not surprisingly, his mouth is flapping.

"That didn't take long," I say.

"What?" he says, but his smirk tells me he already knows.

"You're scum, man," I say, but that's nothing he hasn't heard before. I'm searching every dark corner of my brain for something that will hurt him. I find something I think might work, dust it off, and say: "You and your drunken hillbilly family." I do my imitation of the hillbilly guy on *The Simpsons*: "Garsh, Daisy May, you done pooped out another one. Think I'll call this one Mars, like the candy bar."

Now his eyes narrow, but his smile just gets bigger.

"Be careful," he says, "or I won't have my hillbilly folks drop the lawsuit."

And the way he says that last part, like the words just aren't long enough to contain all the sarcasm he's trying to pack into them, lets me know what an idiot I was to even try, to gamble on that 1-percent chance. It stings a little extra because I let him bait me into it: "We're friends, right?"

And now he's just standing there, grinning at me. I tell myself not to, but I can't help it. I take a quick step forward, my hands coming up as I move. I'm just going to give him a good shove, see how that goes. But before I can, two hands clamp down on my shoulders from behind, strong hands, pulling me up short. I wheel around, and the hands fall away.

It's Aaron. Of course. He puts one hand back on my shoulder, almost friendly, but still controlling me. "Settle down, man," he's saying. "Come on, JD."

I shake his hand off, and this time he lets me. "Stay out of this, man," I say.

He shakes his head. "Can't do it."

This is such bull. I knew he'd take Mars's side. I give Aaron a quick look, confirming what I already know. I can't beat him. Mars starts to say something behind me, almost in my ear, but Aaron shoots him a look and cuts him off: "You too, Mars. You've said enough."

I guess I should be grateful, but I'm mostly just annoyed Aaron is here. I start to walk away just as Rudy arrives. To his everlasting credit, he's pissed on my behalf. Maybe on his own, too. Everyone knows we're best friends, so he's going to get some splatter from Perfumegate.

Rudy is wearing a long-sleeve T-shirt that says JUST DID IT. Our great triumph of second period was convincing Mr. Morill that it's an "inspirational athletic slogan," as evidenced by the poorly drawn Nike swoosh above it. Now he's heading for Mars and has a look in his eyes like he's going to Just Do something violent. I save Aaron the trouble and put my arm out in front of Rudy. "He's useless," I say.

"You might want to pick your friends better," Mars says to him. "Maybe based on something besides" — he pauses, savoring it — "their scent."

"You might want to pick yours better," Rudy tells Aaron.

Now it's like a four-way, crosswise argument. I do the right thing and just walk away. I'm not going to win this battle, and what would it matter if I did? I've already lost the war. Rudy fires a few more individual swears at Mars and then comes with me. We're gone before any teachers arrive.

"Mars is made of dick," says Rudy, as if I'm going to argue.

By lunch, everyone knows. Or at least everyone I know knows. We sit with the Goonies again, or at least we try to. Randall and Jesse are already at a table when we get there. They eye us with suspicion, disgust, or both as we drop our trays, but they don't stand up and leave. But Tal and Junior Goonie First Class Evan spot us early and walk right by the table.

I'm double Kryptonite right now. Juvie basically makes me a delinquent and a lowlife around here. The only people who won't mind that are the tough kids and actual lowlifes, and they'll think the perfume makes me a wimp or worse.

Randall and Jesse don't say much about it. They don't say much at all. Then, right at the end, Randall goes, "Maybe, uh, maybe you shouldn't sit here tomorrow."

"You're pathetic," says Rudy, even though we're the ones left sitting alone.

By the time I get to English I'm so beat down that if I had a car, I'd just cut and go home. But I don't and I'm really wondering how Janie is going to react. She is, after all, the girl I was dating when I went on my now legendary (by Dahlimer standards) crime spree. Some of them will remember the fight and the rest will just speculate — armed robbery? Auto theft? — because everyone knows they don't send you away for your first offense.

I guess she's wondering how she's going to react too, because she just avoids me until class starts. It's easy enough to do, sitting four rows away. Meanwhile, Aaron is sitting on the other side of Rudy again, and the two of them have been rapid-fire whispering back and forth.

Class starts and I finally look at the dry-erase board. Mr. Kibbee is standing there and he slowly and clearly writes: *Smells Like Teen Spirit.* It's the title of a Nirvana song, and I'm thinking: Oh, please don't. But he does. He reads us the lyrics to the song and we have to analyze it as poetry. Some of the kids think it's "unfair to real poetry," but the rest of us understand immediately that it's unfair to the song.

It's debatable, but I consider Nirvana a punk band. Their sound is pretty heavy, and they have lyrics like "I wish I could eat your cancer when you turn black."

Early on, Kibbee asks, "Does anyone know where the title 'Smells Like Teen Spirit' comes from?"

I know the answer, but I don't raise my hand. I figure I'll let Kibbee relive his youth, or whatever he's doing, and tell us himself. But he must suspect that at least one of us knows, and he keeps waiting.

"No one? Really?" he says.

Finally, I raise my hand.

"Yes, JD."

"Teen Spirit was a kind of girls' deodorant," I say. "I think maybe Cobain's girlfriend wore it. Anyway, someone wrote 'Kurt smells like Teen Spirit' on his wall."

Kibbee nods and smiles. "Yes, exactly. Excellent, JD."

For a few seconds, I actually feel kind of good about myself. Then, two rows up, Jefferson raises his hand.

"Yes, Jeff," says Kibbee. To give you an idea of what a teacher's pet he is, the teachers are the only ones who call him that.

"So, a kind of girls' deodorant," he starts. "Is that like perfume?"

Eighty percent of the class laughs. No one is too uncool to get fat off my corpse today.

38

"Wanna kill something?" Rudy says as he drops me off in front of my house. He's asking if I want to play video games. If we were still talking about Mars, he would've said "someone."

"Nah," I say. "Gonna walk the dog."

"Is that what they call it these days?" he says.

The Fiesta drives off with a roar that promises more speed than it delivers. All bark and no bite. JR, who it turns out is some of each, hears it and his head pops up in the window. The muzzle is still hanging on the back of the kitchen door when I squeeze inside. I ignore it and go get his leash from the other room.

The combination of me being home and having the leash in my hand has him wild-eyed and drooly mouthed with excitement. He pauses as I put the leash on and actually sort of drops his head down to let me, but then he's back to whirling around and barking.

I have to make him calm down before we head out. I learned that on *Dog Whisperer*, too. If he bolts out the door with me basically waterskiing behind him, then he's in charge, and he'll expect to stay that way the whole walk. I tug the leash a little, look at him, and go: "Grrrrrr!" He powers down about 50 percent.

I do it again. He looks back at me like ⸢

The brown dots above each eye raise u⸢

God, he sits down.

"Good boy," I say, and we're ready to go.

As soon as the door opens, he nearly pul⸢

socket. OK, so it's still a work in progress. I wor⸢

in as we cross the yard. I'm not sure if I've mentio⸢

weighs close to a hundred pounds, and at least⸢

muscle. "Grrrr!" I say. "Come on, Johnny, GRRRRR!⸢

The growl is supposed to show that I'm the "pack ⸢

my voice breaks so badly on the last one that it soun⸢

squeak toy. JR turns and looks. With that first burst behii⸢

he slows to a trot. I get him down to a walk without too ⸢

trouble, but it is highly debatable who's in charge at this poin⸢

doesn't matter much once we hit the trail.

Until we see the Pomeranian.

It's one of those little dogs — fashion accessories, basically. If
JR is mostly muscle, this thing is mostly fluff, and it looks like a
strong breeze could carry it away. I look down at JR. "Don't even
think about it, boy," I say.

Yeah, sometimes dogs bite people, but most of the violence has
always been dog on dog. I've only been watching the dog pro-
grams on TV for a little while, but I already know that encounters
between yappy little breeds and powerful large breeds are the
Shark Week of the pet world.

"Oh, he's gorgeous!" says the lady holding the fluff ball's leash.
"Is he friendly?"

"Thanks," I say. "Good question."

little dog lets out a few high-pitched yaps. JR opens his wide, and a long strand of drool drops to the ground like ape ladder. Then he snaps off one big "WARRFF!"

he little dog may have a brain the size of a grape, but it knows ugh to stop yapping. The eyes of both dogs are wide open. My scles are super tense. It's not the "calm, assertive energy" I ould be projecting, but I need to prepare for the lunge. An image ashes through my mind, crystal clear in the way that mistakes are afterward: I see the blue muzzle hanging from the doorknob, the metal rings reflecting the light as I open the door.

The lady is wearing a pink warm-up suit and holding a pink leash. Even worse, the Pomeranian is leading her: It's six or seven pounds tops but 100 percent in charge. After a brief pause, the little dog is on the move. It's heading straight toward JR in a series of prancey toy-soldier steps, and the lady is following dutifully along.

"I don't know," I say, and loop the leash around my hand to tighten my grip.

And then the dogs bow to each other. I'm not entirely sure which one bows first, but they're both down there now. Their front legs are flat on the ground in front of them, and their heads are resting on them. JR's butt is still a few feet in the air. The fur ball's is, I don't know, eight inches off the ground. Bowing is kind of redundant at that size.

The lady lets out a delighted laugh. I let out a sigh of relief.

"They like each other!" she squeals.

"Yeah," I say. "Come on, Johnny."

That went pretty well, but I don't want to push it. I pull him away, and he doesn't protest too much. His head turns and follows the little dog as we walk away. He looks back at it, up at me, and back at it again, as if to say: "What was that?!"

"That's a Pomeranian," I say. "They're kind of like fuzzy Chihuahuas. Or fancy rats."

We walk on for a while and I add: "Thanks for not eating it."

We go all the way to the pond and back. JR's been inside all day and needs to burn off some energy. I've been in school all day and need to burn off some anger.

When we get home, I see Mom's car already in the driveway. She doesn't usually get home until after five, so this is way early. I know immediately this isn't going to be good.

39

"Hey, Mom!" I call as I close the door.

The door swings closed and the muzzle slaps against it from its perch on the inside handle, where Mom must've already seen it. I take the leash off JR, but he doesn't scamper out into the living room like usual. He stands there with his mouth hanging open and a low noise coming from the back of his throat. Then he takes a few slow steps forward, and I realize there's someone else here.

"Oh crap!" says Greg, skidding to a halt at the edge of the kitchen.

I grab for JR's collar, but he doesn't go for Greg, just drops his butt down, raises his head, and starts snapping off those sharp, angry barks again.

"SHHHHH!" I say, giving his collar a good tug. "Shut it!

"He's just saying hello!" I shout to Greg over the noise, but what I'm thinking is: Didn't we already go through this? "You surprised him."

"I surprised him?" shouts Greg. "Did you see me jump?"

I think it's true, though, because JR is already calming down. I give his collar another tug and he lets out a few last barks.

"Can I?" says Greg, gesturing toward the refrigerator.

"Sure," I say, digging my hand in deeper under JR's collar. But as soon as Greg opens the fridge, JR loses interest in him and focuses on the open door. He understands it has some connection to food, but I think he's still trying to work out the mechanics of it all. Greg grabs a can of Mom's Diet Coke and swings the door closed again. JR looks from the soda to the door and back again, the wheels turning in his head.

"I didn't see your car," I say. I turn around and look out the window, as if I could possibly have missed such a glaring example of late-stage American capitalism.

"I'm parked downtown," he says. "Thought I'd walk it. Been sitting in court all day. Really technical case. Lots of expert witnesses, very boring. The defense rests, if you know what I mean."

Uncle Greg always talks really fast when he's been in court.

"OK," I say, "so why are you here?"

He's looking at JR, who's watching him drink the soda.

"Oh," he says, lowering the can. "Oh yeah. Dog's much better this time."

"Yeah, he's getting a lot better. Why are you here?"

I can practically see him switching gears, going from uncle to lawyer. I've seen that before, but there's something else. Mom appears in the doorway. She doesn't mention the muzzle, even though she must know I just walked JR without it. "Hey, Jimmer," she says.

Her voice is so sad, and Greg is here and in lawyer mode....

"What's going on?" I say. "Did someone die or something?"

I must know, though, because I look down and realize I'm

standing in between them and JR. It's like I'm trying to shield him from something, or from them.

"Something turned up in discovery," says Greg.

"What?"

"Why don't you come sit down?" says Mom.

"Why don't you tell me right here?"

She exchanges a look with Greg. He takes a sip of Diet Coke and nods. "I'll show you," he says.

We head into the living room. JR splits off and heads for his spot.

"Induction papers for the shelter," says Greg. "Place where you got this guy."

He points the soda can at JR.

"So?" I say.

"Well, apparently he was kind of a handful, is all."

"Let me see," I say.

The papers are on the table. It's just a few pages, and the words are a little fuzzy. It's a printout of a scan of a fax or something like that. I skim it quickly and it doesn't take me long to find the problem.

"What do they know?" I say. "What's 'potentially dangerous' anyway? A stick is potentially dangerous. A bar of soap, a toaster."

"Yeah, well, the thing is, coming from them, that's basically official," says Greg.

"What'd he do," I say, "bite the vet?"

"Or the guys who removed him, or both, or tried to anyway."

"Well, wouldn't you?" I say. "You've been chained to a tree and treated like crap your whole life and here come a bunch of strangers grabbing you and sticking you with needles or whatever? What's he supposed to do?"

I'm getting really upset now, and JR must sense it, because he starts barking again.

"Sit down, OK?" says Mom.

"OK," I say, though it's possible she's talking to JR.

"Want some of my Coke?" says Greg.

"No," I say. "I don't drink diet, or backwash."

"The thing is," says Mom. "I kind of already got him off death row."

"Great job," I say, but she ignores it.

"It's just that by the time I saw him, he was already, you know, him. He was so sweet looking. And you'd just been, well, you were where you were, and I thought, I don't know . . . I thought that he'd be good for you, and maybe you'd be good for him, and you could both get new starts."

"Yeah, right," I say. What a joke. Clean starts are a frickin' myth. His past has followed him just like mine has. And then something else occurs to me.

"You knew this was going to happen," I say. "You knew they'd find out."

"I was afraid they would, yes," she says.

"What about you?" I say, turning on Greg so fast, I catch him mid-gulp.

Kkuh-kuh, he coughs. He wipes his mouth with the back of his hand and says, "Nope. She didn't tell me, either."

"If I told him, he'd have to tell them," she says.

"And it's not like I'm her brother or doing this as a favor or anything," he says.

I look over at JR, spread-eagled in the corner. His head is on the floor but his eyes are following us.

"But they know now?" I say.

"Yep," says Greg. "As one-eight-hundred types go, their lawyer isn't bad."

"So what does it mean?" I say.

"It isn't good," says Greg. "That's kind of, I mean, it's three strikes. It's gonna cost more, for sure, and the insurance company will try to use this to pay less of the more, if you know what I'm saying. They may try to get out of it entirely."

"What about for JR?"

"Well," says Greg. "That's pretty much it."

"What do you mean, 'it'?"

"I mean that's it," he says. "That's all she wrote."

"But he's . . ." I start. "There was just . . . a Pomeranian . . . and plus, with Mars, it was . . ."

They listen to me sputter out half thoughts, and the looks on their faces are more sympathetic than I can take.

"He won't feel anything," says Mom. "And it's better now than before. He just would've died alone."

I have no intention of having this conversation with her.

"How long?" I say.

"It's quick," says Greg. "Just like going to sleep."

He has no idea how long it takes me to get to sleep, and that's not what I mean anyway. "How long do we have?"

"Not long," says Greg, "if we do it. More if we wait for them, drag our feet. It's not going to change anything, though. You don't come off death row twice."

I stand up and leave. JR is probably watching me, maybe even following me, but I can't look back right now or I'm going to lose it. I slam the door behind me and stomp around the front yard for a few minutes. My phone's in my pocket and I take it out and make the call. Rudy answers on the third ring.

"Something bad happened," I say, instead of hello. "We're going to have to do something bad, too."

He doesn't respond right away. I figure he's thinking it over, but then I recognize the faint sound of chewing. He gulps it down and answers.

"You called the right guy."

PART·III

GETTING TO MARS

40

It's easy for Rudy and me to cut school on Wednesday since Rudy's my ride there anyway. It's just a question of what turns you do and don't make after that. We head straight for the nearest Dunkin' Donuts, but the nearest DD is not all that near. It's located between Stanton and Brantley in an area that probably has a name but that we call Stantley. It's the perfect place for a covert operation.

It's midmorning and the place is hopping with coffee addicts. "I'm 'a get some Munchkins," Rudy says as we shuffle toward the front of the line.

"Munchkins?" I say. "What are you, four? Man up and get some donuts."

"No way," he says. "Look. They're having a sale."

He points to a sign for a back-to-school sale on Munchkins. It has a bunch of Munchkins with little faces riding a cartoon school bus.

"When they say, 'back-to-school,' they mean like kindergarten, first grade," I tell him, but he cannot be reasoned with and orders a dozen, along with a coffee.

"Milk and sugar?" says the lady, whose name tag says KIMITHA.

"Light and sweet," he says.

He pauses and I'm wondering, Is he going to say it? And then he does: "Like me."

"You're a loser," I say behind him, but I'm glad he's feeling so relaxed. We're on the verge of doing something risky and maybe dangerous. There's really nothing in it for him, but he's treating the whole thing like some big prank that we're both in on.

No Munchkins for me. I order my chocolate-frosted donuts like a man, dammit, and it's not my fault if they give me the ones with pink sprinkles. I didn't think Kimitha would do that to me. Maybe I shouldn't have ordered my coffee light and sweet, too.

We don't have much trouble finding a little two-person table, since most of these people are getting their stuff to go. And really, what could possibly go wrong trying to drink hot coffee and eat a jelly donut while driving too fast to work?

We plunk our stuff down and look both ways, in case anyone here is trying to spy on us. The coast is clear, and we are now officially ready to plan.

"Got any ideas?" I say.

"Nah," he says. "You?"

"Nothing good."

We start in on our food. Then we try again while we wait for our coffee to cool down a little more. I start with the general mission statement: "The basic thing is, we need to force Mars to do what he said he was going to do anyway. Really, we're just cashing a check he's already written so —" I take another bite of my donut.

"I'd never take a check from Mars," says Rudy. "Can you imagine? He's never going to have viable credit."

I laugh with my mouth full and a tiny fleck of donut shoots off to my left. I'm never really sure if Rudy says things like that to make fun of his parents or because he's been corrupted by all the secondhand realty he's exposed to. I'm not sure he knows, either.

"You know what I mean," I say. "But we really need to motivate him this time, because he'll need to really work on his parents. Or, we can try to work on them, but that's trickier."

"And when you say, 'work on' . . ."

"You know, get something on him," I say.

"And when you say, 'get something on him' . . ."

"What are you, wearing a wire?"

He laughs just as he's taking another trial sip of his coffee and sprays some out the side of his mouth.

"Nah," I say. "No cop is that bad at drinking coffee. Anyway, what I mean is, well, *blackmail* is kind of a loaded word but . . ."

"But blackmail."

"Yeah," I say. "Or *extortion*? Is that better? Maybe not."

"We could plant something on him," says Rudy.

"Dude, this is Mars we're talking about. He's probably got something on him right now."

"Good point. So what do we do, like, a citizen's arrest?"

"I'm not sure we're the right citizens for that."

"Pictures, maybe?"

"Maybe," I say. "But of what?"

"This is harder than I thought," he says.

"Yeah, really."

Our coffee is cooler now, so we spend some time drinking it, looking out the window, and thinking. Or at least the first two of those, because I'm drawing a blank.

"We could beat the crap out of him," says Rudy, after a few minutes.

"We should do that anyway," I say. "Not sure how it helps in court, though."

"We can just be like, 'But, Your Honor, he's a total jerk.' "

We drink the rest of our coffee. This stuff is kind of growing on me.

"You know," I say, "he's probably at school now."

Rudy doesn't understand at first, and then he does. "What about his folks?"

"I think they have jobs, right?"

"Yeah, maybe."

"Yeah, you know, like his dad's at the meth lab and his mom's obviously on the stroll."

"Yeah," says Rudy, already sitting back and getting ready to stand up. "He probably has all kinds of stuff in his room. The whole place to ourselves, lots of potential."

"Yeah," I say, gathering up my stuff. "You know on TV how you see people get busted for growing a bunch of marijuana in their garden or whatever?"

"Yeah?"

"Total DiMartino thing to do."

"Totally."

"Your phone take pictures?"

"Yeah, good ones."

"Mine, too. This is going to be perfect. If we find something like that, it's not even blackmail. It's like, 'You drop the lawsuit or we're going to the police.' It's just a trade."

"It's the American way," says Rudy, nodding.

And just like that, we head off.

"So basically we're on a reconnaissance mission," says Rudy as he pushes through the doors.

"Yeah, it's an intelligence-gathering operation," I say as we step out into the parking lot. Say what you want about our lack of details or clear objectives, but we definitely have the lingo down.

Step one is easy: We just drive around for a while. In the Fiesta, driving slowly is a given, which is perfect. We need to give everyone time to clear out of the DiMartino family residence, which we've more or less convinced ourselves is one of the region's major pot farms, meth labs, and/or porn distributors.

It occurs to me at some point that we should probably be more nervous about this than we are, but we've got too much going for us: caffeine, sugar, and camera phones, mostly.

41

This reconnaissance mission begins, as the best ones do, at thirty-one miles per hour with a bad muffler.

"We should probably . . . not . . . park so close," I say, as diplomatically as possible.

"Yeah," says Rudy. "You're probably right."

The car backfires a few seconds later, just missing its cue. Rudy eases us up onto the grass on the side of the road.

"No one will notice it here, right?" he says as we get out and quietly close our doors. The car is dark green and a few spots of brown rust give it a vaguely camo effect.

"Nah," I say. "It kind of blends."

We walk along the side of the road to Mars's house.

"We probably should've parked at my place and gone the back way," I say.

"Probably," says Rudy.

A car flies by, going about seventy the other way, and we both duck our heads. It's not that strategic to be out here because we are both pretty obviously "of school age." We're both dressed generically, in jeans and sneakers. Rudy is wearing the sort of plain black shirt that I had no idea he even owned, and I am wearing a dark blue T-shirt, the kind with the pocket on the front. As long as we keep our heads down, "two teens in jeans" is not going to narrow the search down much.

We reach the edge of the yard and go into a low crouch. Without even thinking about it, we automatically channel every war movie we've ever seen. We are going to take this bunker! Failure is not an option!

"No cars," whispers Rudy.

"Nice."

"Try the door?"

"Too obvious. Window."

We slip around the side of the house. We're less soldier now, more ninja. We look around the backyard but don't see any vast fields of marijuana or meth lab–looking shacks. There's an upside-down kiddie pool and an old four-wheeler that has only three wheels, but neither of those are crimes.

"Huh," says Rudy.

"Huh," I say. "Let's try his room."

Mars's room has one window, and it's propped up with a removable screen.

"I'll lift the window," I whisper, putting my hand on the frame. "You grab it."

"Got it," says Rudy.

I think he means he's got the screen instead of the idea, and I push the window up. "Don't let it —" I whisper, but the screen has already dropped into the room. It makes a loud, tinny clatter on the floor.

I open my lips and suck in air through my teeth, an involuntary

hiss. Then I slowly duck my head into the place where the screen used to be. As I do, I see the outline of a head doing the exact same thing across the room, peering around the door frame and looking out at me looking in.

"Run!" I say, already turning around.

"What the hell!" I hear someone call out from inside. It's a loud male voice. His head was mostly just an outline to me — and I'm hoping mine was to him — but I figure it's either Mars's dad or one of his frickin' cousins.

"But there was no car!" Rudy huffs as we round the corner of the house.

We are blazing across the front lawn, almost to the road, when the front door slams open behind us. We hear that unmistakable sound: *Shhhuck-shick!*

"Holy crap!" I say, then *BOOM!*

The shotgun goes off behind us. Rudy has never sworn louder or with better reason, but at least it lets me know that he wasn't hit. It's hard to tell, what with my stomach in my chest, my heart in my throat, and my brain trying to get out of my ears, but I think it might've been a warning shot: up rather than at. Either way, we really turn on the jets after that.

We make it off the lawn and to the road without another shot fired. We don't know if the guy is chasing us or what, and I practically tear the door off the Fiesta before I jump inside. Rudy does the same. He jams his hand into his pocket and his keys emerge in a spray of spare change. He finds the right key, jams it in, and turns it.

The car won't start.

Our eyes flick up toward the road in front of us, the corner we just came around at Mach 3. I fully expect to see some dude with a corncob pipe in his mouth and a shotgun in his hands come Confederate-soldiering it around the bend.

"Come on, man," I say. "Come. On."

Rudy is stomping on the gas instead of feathering it, flooding the Fiesta's tiny engine. He realizes it at the same moment I do and lets up on the pedal. The Fiesta coughs and huffs and jerks to life like a guy who was just pulled from a lake. Rudy executes a wild, low-speed U-turn without checking either way.

We don't die, and for a long time, we just drive. Past my house, out of Stanton, past the Dunkin' Donuts. Finally, I say: "Think we lost him."

Rudy pulls into a half-empty parking lot and the Fiesta stalls before he can turn it off. It's not even 11:00 A.M.

42

All afternoon and into the night, I expect to get a call from Mr. DiMartino. If that's who that was, he's known both of us for a long time. Even if he didn't get a good look at my face through the window, there's a decent chance he'd recognize our backs.

Over more or less the same time frame, our failure sinks in. The court date is less than a week away now. I watch a movie called *White Fang* with JR while I'm waiting for Mom to get home. It's about a half wolf, half dog in Alaska or somewhere like that.

"At least you're not half wolf," I say to JR.

He looks back at me with his enormous black-and-brown head.

"Half bear, maybe," I say, but White Fang is back on the screen and JR is mesmerized. His reactions to seeing dogs on TV are hilarious. It's like he suspects they aren't real, but he still can't help turning his head every which way to look at them, raising his ears, and sometimes even barking.

It's not as funny today, since I feel like I might've just gotten him killed, or at least failed to prevent it. I'm 100 percent out of ideas now, and nothing comes to me during the movie. Well, moving to Alaska maybe, but that doesn't seem likely.

Mom gets home a little late, but if anyone called her at work about me, she doesn't say so. She's steering clear because she knows I'm in a horrible mood. She is too, and JR is upset because we are, which just makes it worse. We have grilled cheese sandwiches and tomato soup for dinner, as if one of us is sick.

Rudy calls after that. This is still a crazy adventure to him, and he wants to relive it blow by blow, stall by stall. I understand: It's a lot of excitement for a Wednesday. He does most of the recap. Every once in a while, he'll say, "You know?" or "Remember?" and I'll say, "Yeah, yeah" or "Man" or "Totally."

"Well, all right then," he says, wrapping it up. "Guess I'll pick you up tomorrow?"

"I guess so."

We'd definitely cut school again, if we had any idea what to do with the time. Detention, we'll risk. Getting shot in the back, that's where we draw the line.

"Thanks again, man," I say.

"No problemo," he says and hangs up.

I head to my computer for another round of useless Googling. My chat box launches from my home page, and I see the bubble next to Rudy's name turn green at the same moment mine does. Don't chat too much, dude, I think, but honestly, I don't even care much at this point.

I search dog bite cases for a while, looking for some trick or technicality. But if anything, these cases are even worse than the ones with the broken skylight and hot tea. There's one where an old man was attacked on his own porch, his dog bit the attacker, and the dog wound up getting put to sleep. There's another where a dog was taken away from a family and killed just for being a pit bull in the wrong city — not for *doing* anything but for *being* something. I see that phrase again, *bully breed*, but it's pretty clear the dog isn't the bully in this one.

Pretty soon, I've had enough and start playing Kastle Keep. It's a build-your-empire game where you complete random empire-related tasks, like "construct battlement," by clicking on buttons. It calms me down. Plus, I'm almost at level five hundred.

An hour later, it's pitch-dark out and I *am* at level five hundred. That's pretty impressive, considering I didn't play it at all this summer. We were barely ever allowed online in there, and who's going to spend all that time earning a half hour at the computer just to waste it building a fake empire? That would be sad even by juvie standards. This game is the opposite: for people spending too much time online.

I've got nothing better to do, since I don't know what my homework is. In fact, when Janie pops up on chat, I'm pretty sure that's what it's about. I figure she's going to give me the English homework or warn me about a quiz or something like that. Then I figure she'll give me trouble about ditching school while most of the class is probably still talking about me. It's kind of true too: If you want to let a fire build, you give it space and fuel.

As with pretty much everything I've been sure about lately, I'm completely wrong.

Hey, she writes.

Is 4 horses, I write.

Technically that's one of "our things" and maybe I shouldn't be doing it right now. Then again, it might be bad if I don't.

Where were you? And Rudy?
Trying something
Did it work?
No. Almost got killed.
Melodramatic much?
No srsly

There's a long pause and then **Janie is typing: What were you trying?**

I've heard of chat transcripts being used in court. I don't think Janie would ever do that to me, but I can definitely see my hard drive ending up in court someday. And my Internet provider probably has my records ready to go on a day-to-day basis.

It was about Mars.
He was in school.
Talking all day?
Seems like it
Great

Long pause. **JD is typing: We tried to get something on him.**

That could mean anything, right? Probably shouldn't have used *we*. Sorry, dude.

Like what?

Doesn't matter. Didn't happen.

Bummer. Can you just talk to him?

That's such a girl thing to say.

Didn't work. He's immune.

Goo pt, she types. Good point. I love her typos, and she has never liked Mars. It was actually kind of a problem early on for us. She definitely won that argument.

So what did you do?

Can't say

OK

We tried to get something on him, like some leverage. I shouldn't have typed that, but I sort of want her to say that it was a good idea, that I wasn't being a total idiot.

Like something /incriminating/ :o

Maybe. We tried to get to him but we can't b/c he doesn't care. And his family is heavily armed.

I know how 2 get 2 Mars. . . . she types.

How????

Long pause. **Janie is typing: Go to Venus, turn left.**

Not funny!
Srry

We are going to lose house and dog! Not funny! There's a 90 percent chance that's 50 percent true, but I really need her to know how not funny that was.

Long pause. Now I feel bad. **JD is typing: Sorry. Frustrated.**

It's OK.
You know how Mars is. He won't listen to anyone. Excpet Aaron maybe.

I spot the typo after I send it. I don't like to have typos of my own with her, and this one looks sort of like *ex pet*. And as I'm having that world-shaking thought, she does some real thinking.

Can you get 2 Aaron?

I just look at it for a few seconds. I hadn't thought of that. It's like math: If A can get to B and B can get to C, then A can get to C. Because the thing about Aaron, apart from him being bigger and probably smarter than me, is that you *can* talk to him. You can reason with him. His brain works. And this isn't a word I use often, but if that's the case, maybe his heart does, too.

Thanks! I type. **You're an angel.**

I know, she writes. Then a little smiley face with wings and a halo pops up on the next line.

Ha! I didn't know you had that.
You never called me that before.

I'm an ass. She waits just long enough for me to realize it and then her chat bubble disappears: **Janie is no longer available.** . . . But Rudy is. This time we plan without all the caffeine.

43

"How was the honeymoon?" says Del Posmer from the opposite corner of the lunch table. Rudy and I are sitting here because it's the only place left. A honeymoon is any time two dudes who know each other are conspicuously absent on the same day.

"Beautiful," I say. "Maui, you know?"

"Yeah," says Del. He doesn't speak much.

The first time you see Del, you want to ask: "What are you?" Not to be mean or rude or anything, but just because it's not really clear. He looks a little bit more like a girl than like a guy, maybe 60–40, but then you notice how hairy his arms are. He's pudgy and baby faced, so his age is hard to figure, too.

Of course, he could grow up to be beautiful, manly, and youthful at the same time, and make a fortune playing a sparkly vampire or a tempted angel or whatever. But right now he's hairy, effeminate, and overweight, and I only know he's a guy because he uses the urinal. Now you might be thinking: But that's all superficial. It's not his fault, it's not who he is. And that's true, and there are probably high schools where people would look past it and find the Unique Individual Within. This is not one of those places. At Dahlimer, sitting at this table is like being exiled to a tiny island with a monster on it.

Part of it is self-exile. I actually think Perfumegate is beginning to burn itself out, and we haven't heard anything about what happened at Mars's place. I guess random shotgun blasts are just business as usual out there. Mars himself is down to a few layers of gauze on his hand and no sling in sight. I told him he looked like he was doing "a lot better" when I saw him in the hall this morning. "Still tingles pretty bad," he said.

Rudy and I are talking at a fairly normal volume, which amounts to a whisper in the roaring chatter of the cafeteria. We hear a tray slap down across from us and look up, expecting anything other than what we see: a well-dressed, attractive, and reasonably popular girl.

"So, what laws are you two considering breaking?" says Janie. "And how can I help?"

Rudy stares at her. Then he looks around to see if any other hot chicks will be joining us.

"Hi," I say.

"Don't get bigheaded," she says. "I'm here for the dog."

"OK," I say.

"I can tell you two are up to something over here," she says. "I can always tell when you two are up to something. So what is it?"

Our current plan doesn't call for any actual lawbreaking, but plans change. And you don't want to telegraph your punches, either. My eyes flick over toward Del. "I'll tell you . . . later," I say.

"Do I look like I care?" says Del, his eyes fixed firmly on his food.

"No, but it definitely seems like you're listening," says Rudy.

"Touché," says Del.

He takes one more bite, gathers his stuff, and leaves.

"He didn't have to do that," says Janie.

"Yes, he did," says Rudy.

It's true. Still, it was cool of him, and I kind of make a mental note of it. Then I lean forward and begin telling Janie our plan.

44

School's out and we're going to talk to Aaron. To talk to him and, in JR's case, maybe drool on him. When we were coming up with this so-called plan, Rudy was like: "Dude, I think we have to take the dog. Aaron already knows us — and he prefers Mars. That's pretty damning right there."

And he's right, JR is a lot more lovable than we are. He's a big, doofy, fairly badass dog, and Aaron has been wanting to meet him since day one. The problem is his teeth, and the fact that Aaron looks a lot like his least favorite thing in the world: an adult male. But it's not like we can use the muzzle. It's the Hannibal Lecter thing, the PR. We might as well have him snarling in a cage. And anyway, if he bites him, he bites him. It's not like they can kill him twice.

Our other secret weapon is Janie. I don't know if Aaron really likes my once and hopefully future girlfriend. But I've definitely caught him looking a few times, and I do know she has better people skills than Rudy or me, and her hair smells a lot nicer. Plus, JR is completely in her power.

"Upsy-daisy!" she says, and pats him on the butt. Just like that, he climbs into the tiny backseat of the two-door Fiesta.

"How the hell?" says Rudy.

"Not cool, dude," I say to my dog as his stumpy nontail disappears into the car.

We'd been trying to coax him in there for like five minutes. Now Janie climbs in after him. "It's no problem," she says, gracefully twisting her body through the narrow gap behind the pushed-forward front seat. "I'm Romanian. I come from a long line of gymnasts."

Rudy and I climb into our usual spots and close the doors: *Whump! Whump!* Key in the ignition and, for once, the Fiesta starts right up. It seems like a good omen.

"This is what's called a charm offensive," says Janie from behind us.

"Not if JR bites him," I say. "Then it's just a regular offensive."

"But you won't, will you, boy?" she says to JR in something bordering on baby talk.

He lolls his head over and looks her in the eyes, and she pets him. Right then he looks completely harmless, but she's a girl. "We have an understanding about that," she assures us. And then, to JR, in that voice again: "No biting. No bitey-witing."

Rudy starts backing out of the driveway, and suddenly JR is standing up, sitting down, standing back up, and attempting to turn around in the too-little space. He's going a little crazy at the motion of the car, and even Janie can't calm him down.

"What should I . . . ?" says Rudy.

"Just keep going," I say.

It works. As soon as he shifts into drive, JR's snout shoots over my shoulder, and he sticks his nose out the gap at the top of the window. With a few brief exceptions, he stays like that the whole ride. When we pick up speed, like on the downhills, I can practically hear his gums flapping in the wind. His eyelids are pushed back in a funny way, and every once in a while, flecks of drool hit my face or neck.

"Glad you're enjoying yourself," I say, wiping my cheek.

He ignores me.

And then Janie starts in on the music. "This song sucks," she says. "Why do you two listen to this old junk?"

"What?" I say. "This is Mission of Burma. Total classic."

"Burma's not even a place anymore," she says. "It should be Mission of Myanmar."

"That sounds completely lame," I say.

"Exactly!" she says.

Rudy has his iPod hooked up to the speakers. It's the newest thing in the car by twenty years. The next song reaches the chorus and Janie shouts over it: "Is this the Cookie Monster singing?"

It's Black Flag, which she should know by now, and it's just so unfair. I mean, that's something you could say about the singer from Cannibal Corpse or one of those bands, but not Henry frickin' Rollins.

"I'm sorry," says Rudy. "I don't have any" — he pauses and we all know he's trying to come up with something lame — "Taylor Swift."

We both take a quick look in the mirror to see if that shot landed. What we see instead is that Janie's actually bouncing her head to the chorus: "Rise above! We're gonna rise above!" Rudy and I exchange smirks.

"Oh, please" we hear behind us.

It's a short trip to Aaron's house, even in the Fiesta, and we only get through a few songs before it comes into view. I've done a pretty good job of keeping my nerves in check with the music and wisecracks and all of that, but now my nerves launch a bold and decisive counterattack.

"Well, there's his car," I say.

"And we're sure Mars isn't here?" says Janie.

"Yeah. Detention."

"That didn't take long," she says.

"Never does," I say. I don't mention that I'm supposed to be there, too. I took us both down with a shouting match in the hallway, and now I'll probably get doubled or even tripled up for skipping it. I just hope it's worth it.

Rudy slows the car down as we approach the driveway. JR pulls his head in and retreats to the backseat, drunk and clumsy from too much air. Rudy flicks his turn signal on, nearly unprecedented behavior, and we head up toward the house. The house has a large lawn, which makes for a long driveway. The Fiesta creeps noisily up it, before coming to a slow, shuddering halt behind Aaron's shiny red Malibu.

There's no way Aaron doesn't know we're here. For a second I think: What if he comes bursting out the door with a shotgun, too? I have to remind myself: We're still friends. Yeah, he pulled me away from Mars in the hallway, but he probably did me a favor there. And even with Mars, pretty much everyone thinks we're just feuding. We've all known one another for a long time.

Rudy and I get out of the car. "You got him?" I say.

Janie holds up the end of the leash, and I pull the seat forward. JR climbs out first and shakes his head around, his ears flapping and slapping against his head. Janie climbs out after him, and I push the seat back and close the door.

"That him?" I hear.

I whip around, and there's Aaron. The front door is open, and he's leaning against the frame and eating a slice of cold pizza.

"Yep," I say.

He nods at Rudy. He's sizing us up, trying to figure out why we're here, but he's so frickin' casual about it.

"Hey," he says to Janie, much smoother than I'm comfortable with. Most of the time when I was dating her, I tried to keep those two apart, not because I thought they wouldn't like each other, but because I was afraid they would.

"Hey," she says.

He's chewing again and doesn't answer. Instead, he looks at JR, who is looking at the pizza. But his butt's low. That's bad. I don't know if this is a Rottweiler thing, or if it's just him, but when he really barks, like at Greg, with his teeth snapping and his eyes wide, his butt gets low. Butt low, head high, jaws flapping.

"Don't," I say.

He turns and looks up at me. If he starts barking like that, this is over before it begins. I think Janie knows, too, because she starts scratching him behind the ears.

"He want the pizza?" says Aaron. He raises the hand holding what's left of the slice, then lowers it. JR follows with his head, up, then down. His mouth drops open, but not to bark.

"Huh," says Aaron.

We're about halfway up the walkway, standing in a little group maybe ten feet from him. It's like we're standing there for his inspection, and we're all dressed up for the occasion: me in my black boots, the most punk thing I own; Janie in her extremely tight jeans; Rudy in his most obscene shirt; and JR in the same collar he always wears. Aaron stops chewing for a moment and gives us one last look. He either figures out why we're here or decides he doesn't care.

"Might as well come in," he says, disappearing into the house.

We follow him in, and it's like walking into a cave. It's a fairly bright day outside – partly sunny or partly cloudy, depending on your outlook on life – and there are no lights on inside. Sunlight is streaming in the windows, but it still takes a while for my eyes to adjust.

"The power out?" I say to Aaron, once I locate him again.

"Nah," he says. "I just like to let my eyes cool off after that crap lighting at school. It, like, burns my soul."

"Yeah, I hate those phosphorescent lights," Rudy says, and no one corrects him.

Aaron is standing with his back to a big picture window in the living room. The light is coming in behind him. It's kind of dramatic, like he's an angel or something.

"So, why are you here?" sayeth the angel. "Selling Girl Scout cookies?"

"Well, I know you said a few times you wanted to meet Johnny here," I say, which is true.

"Yeah, and you didn't let me come in that one time," he says.

"He was still really new," I say, shrugging. "Anyway, we were driving around with him — he likes to stick his head out the window. Like in commercials and stuff."

"And you just thought you'd stop by," he says, "and visit your good friend Aaron."

"Yeah," I say. "OK."

"No other motives at all?"

"Yeah, maybe."

It's just me and him talking now. I take a quick look over at JR, to make sure he's not pissing on the carpet or anything. He's sitting down and Janie is down on one knee, scratching behind his ears, trying to keep him calm. Those are some very well-scratched ears at this point, and I wonder if he knows what she's doing.

"You want me to talk to Mars," says Aaron.

I spin my head back around to look at him standing in all that light. In a way, I'm annoyed that it's so obvious, that this whole thing is so obvious. It makes us all seem a little ridiculous, standing here on the edge of his living room, dressed up and pretending to be casual. A little ridiculous and a little dishonest. On the other hand, now I don't have to worry about how I'm going to bring it up.

"Could you?" I say, my tone much more needy than I wanted it to be. I actually hear Rudy wince next to me, sucking in air through his teeth. Aaron shakes his head and smiles at the same time.

"Unreal," he says.

I sort of wonder if this is it, but then Janie says, "Well, you might as well meet him."

Her tone isn't needy at all, just friendly, and his expression resets.

"All right," he says.

He starts walking toward JR. JR stands up, Janie stands up, and I walk around in front of Aaron and on to the other side of my dog. Janie gives me the leash and puts her hand on JR's back. Aaron stops a few feet away.

"Is he friendly?" he says, the universal code for "will he bite?"

"Totally," I say.

"Is he safe?" says Aaron, making sure I got the code. I sort of wonder, and not for the first time, what Mars has told him: the truth, because Aaron is his best friend, or the same story he's been telling everyone else.

"He's way safe," I say.

"What the hell," says Aaron, taking a few steps forward. "That's why they give you two hands."

But I notice he reaches out with his left, the one he's more will-ing to sacrifice. I don't think anyone in the room breathes. Even the breeze that's been blowing in from the hallway seems to stop.

His hand glides down toward JR's head. He pets him.

It's an awkward motion. He sort of pats JR's forehead a few times. It's more like he's blessing him than petting him. Then he pulls his hand back and I exhale.

I look down at JR. He didn't even bark. Maybe it's because I'm right here, or because Janie is, or both. Or if you want to talk about "calm, assertive energy," Aaron cornered the market on that a long time ago. Or maybe he knows this is why he's here. I guess I'll never know. I'm just glad I'm not going through the medicine cabinet right now, looking for more Band-Aids.

"Awesome dog," says Aaron. "Johnny Rotten, right? That's good."

He pauses.

"But I don't know what I can really do for you."

"Did he tell you what really happened?"

"Yeah, he did, and you guys did," he says, looking over at Rudy. "And it's two very different stories."

"He's a rescue, you know?" So, yeah, I trot that out. It's worth a try.

"Yeah, I know. So?"

And then it's like floodgates: "So he had it rough, all right? Like, his whole life, and so maybe he bit Mars, who basically made him, but he was kicked around his whole life and never had a chance to learn anything else. He never had a chance, and now that he does, it's going to be taken away. By frickin' Mars. He's going to be frickin' killed."

"That really going to happen?" he says.

"Yeah, probably," I say. "Because it's up to the judge and there's all this crap that Mars and them are stacking on top of the mountain of crap they're going to wheel into court, just to try to get more money. And, so, dead dog, and he never had a chance, and you don't even know what that's like."

I want to make the point that he's this big, square-jawed dude with a nice car and what does he know about getting the short end of anything, but all I can think to do is point at him. I'm basically accusing him of being himself.

"All right, JD, settle down," he says. "I know what it's like."

"Yeah, how?" I say.

Aaron takes a step toward me, and I feel JR shift on his leash.

"Hey, hey," says Rudy, his first words this whole time.

"Come on, guys," says Janie.

"Because I had a dog," says Aaron.

All I can think to say is "Really?"

"Yeah, I had him from the age of, like, a few months to three years, I think," he says. "Because I got him for my sixth birthday, so yeah, three."

"What, like, what happened to him?" I say.

It's a question I should either definitely ask or definitely not ask, but it's out of my mouth before I can figure out which.

"He just didn't make it, all right?"

"All right."

"That, right there, is never having a chance."

"Yeah, damn. Sorry, man."

"Sorry," says Janie.

"That blows," says Rudy.

Aaron looks at him, then back at me. "So I understand, all right, but I still don't see what you think I can do."

"You could talk to him," I say.

"So could you," he says.

"I have, plenty. But he'd listen to you."

"Wouldn't matter if he did," says Aaron. "His folks — his mom — they're driving that train. They smell money. He's just the one that got bit. And he did get bit."

"Yeah, but Mars provoked him, and there's no way that nerve stuff is real."

Aaron shrugs.

"And you could . . ."

"I could what?" he says.

"Well, if you, like, cut him off, I mean, he's got no one else at school. At least not without you."

"So you want me to cut him off?"

"No, you just need to, you know, act like you might."

"So threaten him?"

"Yeah, why not? Or even do it for a few days. It's his *social* life. This is an actual one."

"Or if you got him to admit it, that he got himself bit, that the nerve stuff is crap," says Rudy.

"Yeah, or that!" says Janie.

They think I'm flubbing this and need their help, but I was getting to that part.

"Admit it to who?" says Aaron.

"Um, a witness?" I say.

Aaron is quiet for a few long seconds, and then he says, "I don't know about a witness, but you might want to get a clue."

The line hits me hard, and Aaron walks it back a little, saying he was just kidding. But I feel stupid, and a few minutes later, we're out in the driveway.

"That could've gone better," says Rudy.

"At least he didn't bite him," says Janie.

"Not like it matters," I say, but I reach down and pat JR's side.

"You don't think he'll do it?" she says.

"What, talk to Mars? You heard him. Wouldn't matter if he did."

"It might," she says.

I hand the leash over to Janie and open the passenger-side door. JR hops right up into the backseat.

"He was so good," I say. "What a waste."

45

Friday sucks – and it's Friday, so that's saying something. For someone who mostly listens to punk rock, with some metal thrown in, my life has been pretty damn emo lately. First of all, there's school. Aaron gives us the cold shoulder all day. If anything, it seems like he's hanging with Mars even more. I see the two of them huddled up and talking about something a few times. I figure he's telling Mars about us stopping by like charity cases, imitating me: *"Could you?"*

God, I feel like a loser. And then I find out my detention got doubled. Skip one day, get two. I think about skipping it again just to see how many days I'd end up with. Instead I go and just sit there, staring at an open book.

We're not even allowed to have headphones in here. That's a double kick in the groin, because you can't listen to music and you can't not hear the whispering around you. Today, it's about me: still the perfume thing. The guys in the back of detention are to gay jokes what microwaves are to cooking.

It's Jordy and those guys. Mars isn't there, which is a good thing. If he was I might end up with a lot more than two detentions. But he served his time yesterday, and I'm left trying to ignore these three goons.

Now they're on to shower jokes, which I guess is about juvie. They consider me a fake tough guy because my classes are a level up from theirs, and I consider them fake tough guys because they're fake tough guys. I know before they do that they're going to get sick of me ignoring them. I wait for the first balled-up piece of whatever to hit the back of my head, and I don't have to wait long.

Once it's over, I have to ride the late bus with two of the same guys, not Jordy but the Jordettes. I've been asking Rudy for a lot lately, and coming back to school on a Friday just to pick me up is too much. Anyway, those two don't say another word. I guess two-on-one is a little too close to a fair fight for them.

I get off the bus and there's Greg's car behind my mom's in the driveway. Now it really is a greatest hits collection. He must've just gotten here, because halfway to the door, I can hear JR still barking at him inside.

I dump my stuff on the kitchen table and the barking stops. Mom pokes her head in the room. "Hey, Jimmer, can you come in here for a sec?"

"Course," I say, but I'm thinking: Uh-oh.

"Hey, Greg," I say, before I even see him.

When I do, he's sitting at the head of the table, like he's going to carve a turkey. JR has retired to his corner, but his head pops up as I walk by. He gives me a look I can't figure out, happy, sad, afraid, maybe all three.

"Pull up a chair," Greg says, as if this is his house.

Mom pulls her chair out slowly and sits down, like she's demonstrating how it's done. She hasn't even asked where I was and why I had to take the late bus. I do my part and sit down.

"Yeah?" I say. The court date is Monday, so I don't know if this is a pregame or what. It's not: The game's over. Greg makes it quick, I guess because Mom already knows. It's official; we're settling. Of course we are. He's been "talking to their guy all day," and they're "willing to settle" for a "significant payout."

"What's that mean for us?" I ask.

"We're going to take a hit," he says.

"What about the insurance?" I say, but I feel like I'm going through the motions here. We already lost, and now I'm just asking for the final score.

"Tried to back out, made a bunch of noise because they weren't told about the earlier incidents," he says. "Which is crap, of course. I rattled their cage a little. It's not my first time with them. Anyway, that's what we're left with. They're paying most of it."

"So we're paying what?"

"The rest."

"Of a 'significant payout'?"

"Yes."

I want to ask him how significant, but I look over at Mom and her expression gives me a pretty good idea.

"And Johnny?"

"Well, I'm not the judge, and I'm not in his head," he says, not answering.

"But?"

"But that ship has sailed. I'm not even sure he has any latitude at this point. We're past three strikes."

I look over at JR, just the top of his back visible from here. I stand up. There's an empty mug on the table in front of me and I pick it up.

"So we're probably going to lose this place?"

Greg and Mom look at each other.

"We might," she says.

"Well then," I say, and throw the mug clean through the window. The mug blows out one of the square glass panes and keeps going. Greg and Mom both flinch, but they don't say anything. JR scrambles to his feet and starts barking.

"Come on, boy," I say over the top of him. "Let's go for . . ."

But I don't say, "a walk." I can't. He gets so happy when I do, and that doesn't seem fair. He figures it out once I grab the leash anyway.

46

"Greg killed you, boy," I say, once we make it to the path. It's a breezy day, and the wind is pushing through the tops of the trees. The rustling sound it makes seems to go on forever. No one else will ever hear what I say now. "Yes, he did, because he's a coward and a bean counter, and he's afraid to go to court."

I don't know if that's true. He says it wouldn't change any-thing, except cost us more money. And I'd say that it feels better to have someone to blame, but nothing about this feels even remotely good. It doesn't matter at all now, and JR has no idea what I'm talking about anyway.

He's sniffing around, tugging on his leash. He loves it out here, and that's killing me. Because it's not so much to ask, right? Except it is, and I'm not even going to be able to come out here after he's gone. I guess I didn't come out here much before we got him, but it still sucks.

I said JR doesn't understand what I've been saying about Greg, and that's true, but he knows I'm upset. He slows down until he's behind me a little and then comes up and bumps the back of my knee with his head. I don't know why he does it that way, but I know what he means. I sit down on the ground, in the grass and dirt just off the path, and he sits down with me.

I don't say anything, and I don't cry, if that's what you're thinking. We just sit there, and after a few minutes, he puts his head on my leg. Two cyclists zip by, and I don't know what they think of us, but I know I don't care.

After that, we get up and head to the pond. Ever since Rudy and I fed him that fish, JR pretty much insists on going all the way there. Then we head back. The wind picks up and it's like it's pushing us home. The tops of the trees are really whipping around, there's no one else here, and now I really can say anything. I only manage two words: "Sorry, boy."

Mom has some words of her own for me when I get inside. "You're being a brat," she says. "You think you're the only one this affects?"

"No," I say.

I get out of the room fast, but she follows me down the hall.

"It's my house, too," she says. "My money, my dog. My window."

She's being generous: It is pretty much entirely her house and money. The dog is debatable, and the window is shattered.

"I know," I say. "Fine. I'll pay for the window."

"With my money."

She's got me there, but I don't regret it. I'm supposed to take a shot like this and what, say "thank you"? I spend the rest of the night watching TV in the front room with JR. Every time he tries to leave, I bribe him with more food. By nine, he's stuffed so full, he barely even moves. He's asleep on his side by the time I turn off the TV and head upstairs.

I sleep for crap and wake up to the sound of Mom's car starting in the driveway. I get up fast and throw on yesterday's clothes. It's Saturday morning, and I don't even know why I'm rushing at first. My brain is still foggy, but something's taking shape in there. I take the first few stairs at a walk and the last few at a run.

I'm in the living room now. "Johnny?" I say. "Hey, boy!"

He's not in his corner. I look down the hallway and check the kitchen. Nothing. Through the kitchen window, I see Mom's car lurch into reverse. I shoot through the door and into the yard. The grass feels cool and damp under my bare feet.

"Stop," I shout, but she already has.

She has to; there's another car pulling in behind her. I recognize it — a big boat of a thing — but it's strange to see it in the driveway. He usually parks it along the curb. I guess he plans to get out this time.

Mom gets out of her car, and I can see she's a little confused, and then Aaron gets out of his. Both doors slam closed at the same moment, and that sets JR off barking in the backyard. He's in the backyard.

"Morning, Mrs. Dobbs," says Aaron.

"Morning, Aaron," she says, not correcting him on the *Mrs.* thing.

"I hear you're harboring a known fugitive," he says.

"I think I'm harboring two," she says.

"Can I speak to the one with two legs?" he says.

"Can you let me out first? I have a meeting at the bank." She says it to him, but she looks at me during that last part.

"Sure," he says. "Sorry, I usually park along the side there."

"Hey, man," I say.

He nods, and then I wait while both cars pull out. Aaron backs his into its normal spot on the edge of the lawn. By the time he gets out and heads toward me, I still have no idea what he's doing here.

"Got a sec?" he says when he reaches me.

"Got all day," I say. "What's up?"

He reaches into his pocket and fishes out a smartphone that looks a lot like mine. "Got something for you," he says.

47

"That my phone?" I say. Aaron and I have the same model, and I think mine is upstairs in the charger but it's too early to swear to it. I see Mom over his shoulder, shifting from reverse into drive and heading down the road.

"Wake up, man," says Aaron. "I didn't come here to give you a phone. It's way better than that."

"Yeah?" I say, trying to focus. "What?"

He shakes his head, disappointed. He wants me to guess, but I have no idea. "Dude, man, I got nothing," I say.

He looks at me, like: You sure? I just stand there like an idiot and he gives up.

"A witness, man," he says. "I got your frickin' witness."

Now I'm awake. "What?" I say. "Who?"

"Me," he says, holding his phone up higher, "and my little friend."

He turns the phone back around and touches the screen a few times. Then he holds it out to me.

I hear Aaron's voice: "But you did hop the fence, right? I mean, you were kind of asking for it."

The next voice is Mars: "What, screw you! I reached over first, but he kept backing away. Seemed more scared than anything. So I hopped the fence. I always do."

"And you just kept after him? Dumbass!"

"Yeah, I guess it was kind of, like, he wasn't exactly growling, but he was showing some teeth — big teeth!"

"And you stuck your hand in there anyway."

"Yeah! I thought he'd stop, like I'd win him over with my awesome petting!"

"Dumbass!"

"Yeah!"

Aaron lowers the phone. And now it's his voice, for real. "Did you even know these things have an audio recorder?"

"Yeah, but I never used it," I say. "My mom uses hers to make, like, little notes to herself about work and stuff. . . ."

"Yeah," he says. "I still don't think Mars knows."

I smile. I can't help it.

"You boned him, man!"

"Yeah," he says, looking away. "Feel bad, but it's all on here. Have another one about the nerve damage thing."

"And it's crap?"

"Course it is."

"Wow," I say. "Wow. You, uh, want to come in, see the beast?"

"Sure."

We head for the living room.

"Happened to the window?" he says.

"Threw a mug through it," I say.

He nods, like that's the most normal thing in the world.

"Was that the dog out back?"

"Yeah, I'll go get him," I say. "Want to show you something."

"All right," he says, and walks over to look at the broken window.

JR bumps his way in through the back door and trots into the room, but he stops cold when he sees Aaron.

"For the record," says Aaron, "I could tell you all thought he was gonna bite me the other day."

"No, no," I say, heading to the kitchen. "We just thought he *might.*"

"Well, that's reassuring," he says.

I come back with two biscuits.

"Watch this," I say.

I hold one up, and JR whips his head around toward it. Then I toss it to him. He jumps up and snatches it out of the air, as usual.

"Nice!" says Aaron.

"Yeah, it's like his party trick," I say. "Here, you try."

"Cool," he says, taking the other biscuit. "What, just . . ." he says, making a tossing motion.

"Yeah, throw it high. Anywhere in the general vicinity will do."

The toss is so high, it almost hits the ceiling, but it's really accurate. JR gathers his legs underneath him like a toothy kanga-roo, then launches himself straight up and terminates the biscuit in midair.

"He's like a missile defense system," says Aaron.

"Seriously."

Neither of us says anything for a few moments. We just watch as JR finishes chewing and licks his lips.

"Thanks, man," I say, finally.

Aaron shrugs, but I can't let it go at that.

"This is huge. I really . . . I didn't think . . . I mean, you called me clueless."

"Yeah." He lets out a little laugh and I don't even mind. "You were kind of all over the place. Sorry about that."

"No, it's true, but I mean . . ." I mean, why?

He takes one last look at JR. "I'll tell you something," he says.

"OK."

"Remember I told you I had a dog?"

"Yeah."

"Well, there's a little more to it. His name was Woolly, really Woolly Bear, but we called him Woolly. He was just a puppy when I named him, and I don't think I realized his fur wasn't always going to be that soft. Anyway, he got sick. Nothing too major, but the treatment was gonna be a couple hundred bucks. I remember that seemed like so much money to me then. I was nine, you know? So, yeah, I was nine, he was three, and he got sick."

"Sorry, man."

"Nah, that's not it. My dad didn't want to pay."

"What?"

"Yeah, he didn't want to pay for the treatment, so he had him put to sleep. I guess it cost less, and he'd been out of work for a while. That's why we moved to Stanton. He got a good job here. Anyway, my dog goes to the vet to get some medicine and he just never comes back. If I'd known, I never would've let him go."

"Damn, man. That's just . . . crazy."

"So after you guys left, I was thinking about that. I was thinking, if I had Woolly back and they tried to take him from me again. I'm bigger than my dad now, you know?"

"I know, but . . ."

"But that's the thing. I'm not getting my dog back. It doesn't work that way. But you've still got yours. And Mars is my friend – the first friend I made when I came here – but I'll be damned, you know? I'll be damned if I'll let that happen again."

I don't really know what to say. JR is still standing there, looking at Aaron, but it seems like he's looking at him differently now. Part of that is probably because Aaron gave him a biscuit, but I think most of it is because JR has that radar for when people are upset.

"Thanks, man," I say.

"De nada," he says. We had Spanish together last year.

"Sorry about Mars."

"He'll get over it."

"I guess."

"You don't give him enough credit, you know? He's had it worse than any of us, by a mile."

"I know," I say, though I guess I'd never really thought of it that way before.

"I know you, JD. You think your life's so hard. But you should try sitting through a dinner at his place. And he's still up for anything at any time, and always joking around."

"OK," I say.

"And you might not want to believe this, but I don't think he really wanted to do any of this."

"I kind of do want to believe that," I say. "But he didn't have to tell everyone about . . ."

Aaron shrugs again. "And you don't have to look down on him so much. He hates that hillbilly stuff. And anyway, who cares?

You won. And you're not going to lose any friends over that other stuff unless you want to. All right?"

"Yeah, OK," I say. I think he might be right.

"Good, because I expect you and Rude Boy back in action on Monday."

"What, at lunch and stuff?"

"Just in general."

"Yeah, no problem, man. But, uh . . ."

I point to his phone.

"I'll send you the audio files. Then you do whatever you have to."

"I'll send 'em to our good-for-nothing lawyer," I say. "Even he can't screw that up."

"Whatever," says Aaron. "Let me know if you need me to do anything else. See you Monday, JD. Later, Rotten."

And then he's gone, and I'm standing in my living room, bare-foot and dumbstruck.

"Damn, boy," I say to my dog. "That was a sad story."

Which doesn't explain why I'm smiling.

48

And Greg doesn't screw it up. I know I've said a lot of stuff about him, pretty much all of it negative, but I'll say this for him: He answers his e-mail right away, and he knows what to do with hard evidence. He loads those files up like he's sliding a bullet into a gun, says Aaron is willing to testify to all of it, and kills the case dead. He even asks us if we want to countersue.

"We just want to be left alone," says Mom.

"Well, I can guarantee that," he says. "And you raise that fence out back another foot and put the muzzle on if you take him downtown, at least for now, and we won't have to have this conversation again."

And what kind of fool would say no to a deal like that?

49

The car pulls into the driveway so quietly that only JR hears it. He trots past me and props himself on the kitchen door so that he can see out the window. I get up from the table and stand behind him. He recognizes Janie's hybrid as it bumps to a stop, so he doesn't bark. But she's become one of his favorite people and he has to do something, so he lets out this weird little noise from the back of his throat, basically a bunch of *E*s with some consonants thrown in. It is only by a supreme act of willpower that I don't do the same.

Instead, I fix my hair.

"How do I look, boy?" I ask.

Still propped up on the door, he turns his head and gives me a deeply unimpressed look, like: My hair is better.

She's making her way across the yard now, and I check the present in my hand. It's not wrapped, exactly, but it's in a gift bag and I stuck a red bow left over from last Christmas on top. It looks a little makeshift, to tell the truth, and it's just a dinky little present, but that's OK. I don't want to overdo it. This is supposed to be our first date. We're starting over completely. It was her idea, but I liked it immediately. The truth is, not telling her where I was this summer, or why, well, that wasn't my first mistake with her. The truth is, at least, I hope it is, I really can do better.

"Get down, boy," I say, tugging him away from the door by his collar. "Give the lady some space."

He makes a raspy huff that I now recognize as the Rottweiler equivalent of "Oh, all right," and drops down to the floor. Not really having a tail, he's wagging his whole rear end.

"Hey, guys," says Janie as she pushes the door open and steps inside.

"Hey," I say. "Hi."

She goes straight to JR and starts scratching his fur with her fingernails. He rolls over on the kitchen floor like the big ham he is.

"I got you something," I say, possibly trying to steal some of my dog's thunder. He looks up to see why the belly scratching has stopped.

"Oh yeah?" Janie says, standing up.

She takes a few steps toward me. JR is still on his back, following her with his eyes: But why has the belly scratching stopped? I hand her the bag.

"Nice," she says. "You wrap this yourself?"

I look down at the Christmas bow. The year-old adhesive is already starting to peel away from the bag. "Santa helped me," I say.

She reaches into the bag and pulls out a small stuffed gorilla. She likes gorillas.

"Aw," she says. "He's cute."

"Reminds me of your dad," I say. "Not the cute part, I just mean all the hair."

She makes a sour expression: "Sometimes, you know, it's better not to say anything."

"OK," I say.

She turns the little gorilla around in her hands to get a better look at it.

"It's nice," she says. "Wait, you did pay for this, right?"

"Yeah," I say, smiling, "but I stole the tiny bottle of perfume it's wearing."

"Well, it's nice," she says. "Thank you."

She goes to put it down on the kitchen table.

"Don't," I say. "He might eat it."

JR is on his feet now, staring at this thing, which looks a little like a tiny squirrel.

My mom pops her head into the kitchen to say hi to Janie, but she has the good sense to keep it quick.

"Well, I'll leave you alone," she says, holding up a book. "I'm in the middle of a mystery."

"You know," I say, once Mom's gone, "if you let me drive, it counts as practice toward my license."

"I'm not letting you drive on our first date," she says. "Lord knows where you'd take us!"

"All right then," I say. "Where are we going?"

"The mall," she says.

"Classy," I say, but they actually have some nice restaurants there. "I'm ready. Got my good boots on."

Janie looks down at them and rolls her eyes. It gives me the opportunity to really look at her for the first time tonight. She's wearing good jeans and a nice white top that I've never seen before.

"You look . . ." I say. She looks beautiful.

"I know," she says.

She puts her hand on the doorknob, and JR makes one final, valiant attempt to keep her there: He flops back down onto his back like he's been shot.

"Bye, Johnny," she says, and heads out the door.

He gets up. Now he wants to come with us.

"Not this time, boy," I say. "Go help Mom with her mystery."

It's a cool night out, the first hint of fall creeping into the air. We listen to her music the whole trip over to the far side of Brantley, and I don't complain once. Once we get to the mall, I let her pick the restaurant. And I know you're thinking: Oh, you're being way nicer than you would on a real first date. But this is exactly how nice I'd be, because I'd still be under the delusion that it might lead to something tonight. In any case, she chooses Olive Garden. There's a little music store on the way.

"Let's just take a look," I say.

She doesn't exactly disagree, so we head in. The place has a few sad racks of dusty CDs and some boxes of "vintage vinyl," but it's mostly full of T-shirts, posters, iPod covers, and things like that.

Just past the lame hip-hop section is a small corner devoted to punk and metal, forced together like two unpopular kids at a party. I head straight there and Janie follows along, just to humor me. There are two head-and-neck mannequin tops that weren't here last time. They probably got them from a jewelry store that went out of business.

The male one has a black Misfits beanie on its head and a red skull-pattern bandanna wrapped around its pale plastic neck. It's sporting fake safety pins that clip on instead of through its ears and are pretty much the least punk thing I've ever seen. The female one is dressed about the same, but it does have one cool thing.

"What do you think?" I say to Janie, pointing to the collar around its neck. It's made of black leather and ringed with dull metal spikes.

"I would *never* wear something like that," she says.

I reach out and unfasten it.

"Who says it's for you?"

ABOUT THE AUTHOR

Michael Northrop's first novel, *Gentlemen*, earned him a *Publishers Weekly* Flying Start citation for a notable debut, and his second, *Trapped*, was named an ALA/YALSA Quick Pick for Reluctant Young Adult Readers, an ALA/YALSA Readers' Choice List selection, and an Indie Next List selection. His recent middle-grade novel, *Plunked*, was selected for the New York Public Library's 100 Titles for Reading and Sharing. Michael has also written short fiction for *Weird Tales*, the *Notre Dame Review*, and *McSweeney's*. An editor at *Sports Illustrated Kids* for many years, he now writes full-time from his home in New York City. You can visit him online at www.michaelnorthrop.net.